Elements & the Fae

Elemental Series Book 2

Jillian Beane

Jillian Beane LLC

ISBN: 979-8-9900217-2-3 (eBook)

ISBN: 979-8-9900217-3-0 (Paperback)

Library of Congress Control Number: 2024912661

Book Cover by Shawnna Sue

Paperback Wrap by Jillian Beane

Editing by Dayna Hart at Hart to Heart Edits

1st edition 2024

Jillian Beane LLC

PO Box 10

ELEMENTS & THE FAE

Mechanicsburg, OH 43044

Contents

Pronunciation Guide

Suleima - SUE-LAY-EE-MA

Erist - i-WRIST

Dynasira - dyna-SEE-ra

Dirrin - DEER-in

Kaly - KAY-lee

Hamanad - HA-ma-nad

Yanima - ya-KNEE-ma

Zenisa - ZEN-eesa

Vorelar – vor-EH-lar

Zia - ZEE-ya

Agron - ag-RON

Xiala - zeye-a-LA

Lysom - LIE-som

Sumar - sue-MAR

Kylin - KEYE-lin

Solisa - SO-leesa

Nuckelavee - NUH-klaa-vee

Prologue

THE GROUP HUDDLED TOGETHER around the table. Suleima stood back a moment, taking in the scene. Two werewolves, two dragons, a jinn, and two shamans surrounded the table, looking expectantly at her. It still baffled her that they had chosen her as their de facto leader. The ragtag group was the beginnings of a council who would create and impose rules and punishments over the supernatural community, so no group would be able to attempt to rule over any other again.

Suleima dropped a large chunk of obsidian onto the table, "I found this in the dirt near Dirrin's cabinet. It contains the energy signature of a powerful magic user, but not Dirrin. It feels familiar yet foreign. This was the only clue we found near or in his tent."

Agron, a dragon from Clan Verana, spoke, the extreme bass of his voice grabbing everyone's attention. "We have kept a constant patrol over and around Dirrin's army's campsite. No one has come or gone from the area since it was located."

Suleima nodded. "We need to keep it that way, at least until the remainder of the camp is cleaned up."

"I sent a group of wolves to help tear down tents and structures already marked safe by the shaman. They'll steer clear of the rest, until Suleima or another shaman deem them safe," Gage, the alpha werewolf, added.

Dynasira, leader of Clan Azula and Suleima's best friend, added, "Clan Rojada is housing the prisoners from the battle. Those who have shown remorse are being counseled. Their punishment will be mitigated based on the guidelines the council agreed to. Those without remorse have had their powers bound and are being held awaiting our final sentencing. All remaining bodies have been collected and burned."

Just before the meeting adjourned, Agron spoke up. "I think we need an official name for this council. It will take time for news of us to spread throughout the community, but I think it will go farther and faster with an actual name; not just calling it 'the council.'"

Nods of agreement went around the table.

Lysom, one of the other shaman stood, "Although I didn't know him personally, I have heard a lot of tales of Erist, and obviously, I have met you, Suleima, his student. His kindness and his willingness to work with others from dragons, jinn and many others, and his belief that everyone is equal regardless of their background serves as an example of what we have all agreed this council should do. I propose we should be known as The Council of Erist."

Suleima covered her mouth with her hand, stunned at his suggestion. She made a move to protest. This was not just a council of shaman, although she felt honored at the suggestion.

Hamanad interrupted before she could voice her concern. "I second that. I did have the pleasure of knowing Erist personally. I agree with Lysom's assessment of Erist's character, and before Suleima protests, as I know she is about to," he winked at her before continuing, "It is not Erist's abilities as a shaman which we honor him with by calling this The Council of Erist. We honor Erist and what he stood for as a supernatural."

"I agree." Dynasira stood next to Agron, followed by each of the other council members. Dynasira looked around the room and declared, "The Council of Erist it is!"

Chapter 1

Suleima sat in her cabin deep in the woods, pouring over books and wracking her brain to figure out why the magic residue from the obsidian rock seemed so familiar. She absently rolled it around in her hand.

Suddenly, she dropped the rock to the floor.

She knew.

But how was it possible? Kylin died years ago, before Erist's death.

She pulled out an old book, well used, but well cared for. Erist kept a shaman mentorship 'family tree', listing the mentors he trained with and each of the students they mentored. Once a mentor or student died, their name changed colors.

She traced her finger down the list of names, stopping when she reached Kylin. The name was silver, as it should have been, but there was a sheen to it which didn't match the names of the other shaman who had passed. What did it mean? Kylin had been young when she died, too young to have had any students or children to pass her abilities onto.

Having just dealt with Dirrin's necromancers, she knew death was not always final, but Kylin's ability to manipulate the elements would have died with her.

Suleima closed the book, laying it gently on the table. She walked out onto her porch, calling a small pigeon nearby, wrote a short note, and sent for Dynasira.

Returning to her cabin, Suleima replenished her magic stores. Since the last battle, when she could speak to Erist, and he showed her how to siphon her power, she relied less and less on the Ritual of Alucenia to recharge her power. The time between using her power and recharging it was growing.

Suleima pulled a few books from the chest beneath her bed; most were slightly charred from the fire. They were Erist's journals. The familiar writing made her smile. He was always so organized and precise; it was easy for her to flip to the time surrounding the death of Kylin.

Early in her training, Suleima and Erist had traveled to a meadow near the house of Sumar and Kylin.

Kylin would practice controlling fire, while Suleima would test out her skills with earth, using the dirt to smother Kylin's flames. Erist also encouraged Suleima to practice with her secondary strength with water, trying to pull from a distance the energy from the river.

The only water she ever pulled was from her skin, because she was trying so hard she was sweating. Kylin and Dirrin would team up against her during those sessions, coming at her from both directions with their fire. During those sessions, she learned to shield herself with earth.

Erist's notes did not mention much about Kylin. Only that Sumar stepped away from mentoring. His other wards were reassigned to other mentors, and Sumar retreated to his lake house. She flipped and searched through the journals, but if Erist knew the location of the lake house it was not listed in this journal.

Chapter 2

An hour or so later, a buzz alerted her that her wards were being breached by Dynasira. She stood, stretching her back and headed out to the porch to meet her friend.

After a quick greeting, Suleima explained what she'd learned. "I need to find Sumar. I have no idea where Kylin was laid to rest, but we need to find out if her remains are still there."

"Did you travel outside of Setura when you went to visit them?" At Sulemia's nod, Dynasira continued, "Do you know which direction you traveled? Or the length of time it took?"

"I was still young. I don't remember much. It took a few hours to get to his house, but I'm not sure how many. Erist would usually have Dirrin and I studying through most of the trip. I believe we traveled east. I remember that early in the morning, the sun would be nearly blinding in front of us as we traveled, so I didn't mind burying my nose in a book to keep from being blinded by the sun."

"It's a start. I'll send a scout in that direction and see if they can find any information."

"I'll try to contact people who could have known Sumar or Kylin. Maybe one of them will be able to help narrow it down."

Birds sent to the various shaman who might know Sumar, Suleima headed out into the forest to clear her head. She needed to re-center herself and prepare to take on whatever challenge was about to rear its ugly head. She felt it coming. The energy and pulse of danger were palpable.

She stopped at a gnarled old tree. To the naked eye, the tree appeared dead. No leaves on its spindly branches, and a haunting face in its bark. But the pulse of life inside this tree called to her. It felt what she did: coming danger. She desperately wanted to keep danger away from Amber Mountain. Her presence caused the danger here before. She didn't want anyone or anything from her past to put this place in danger again. Her friends were here. People she cared about.

As if conjured by her thoughts, Suleima sensed Gage's presence. He was on two feet as he approached, and she couldn't sense any of his wolves nearby. The forest around them quieted as the animals in the area sensed the presence of a predator in their midst.

He smiled at her as he came into view, and she couldn't help but smile back. "Hey," he said.

"Hey." She tried to sound more cheerful than she really was, but it must not have been convincing because the smile dropped from his face.

"What is wrong?" he asked.

"I'm not sure." She stopped in front of him, his blue-gray eyes drawing her in. "I feel overwhelmed and restless and now..."

His thumb traced lazy circles on the back of her hand, both comforting and distracting her.

"There is so much to do. So much to clean up after Dirrin. The Council. And now this looming threat I feel. I don't want to be responsible for bringing danger to this place again."

He turned her to face him, dropping her hand and taking her face in his hands, looking directly into her eyes. "You are not alone in this. We're here to help you. Dyna, myself, my pack and the council. We'll take one thing at a time. And we will take care of it. Together.

"You aren't responsible for the danger Dirrin brought. It would've come here eventually without you, and it would have been so much worse. We had you here to help us stop it. It doesn't all fall on you. You were chosen as the leader of our council, yes. Because you brought us together to defeat an impossible power. I have no doubt you will do the same again, if or when another situation arises. I'll be here to support you in whatever you need. You only need to ask."

She held back tears as she smiled at him. "Leave it to you to make it sound so easy, and to make me sound so powerful and brave."

"You are more powerful and braver than you know. I know it. Dyna knows it. My pack knows it. As do the rest of the council. We'll be right here to remind you of it and to give you whatever you need. You are special to all of us. We wouldn't be what we are today without you."

"You make me sound like I could do anything."

"Because I believe you can. And you'll ask for help when the time comes. I'll be the first in line to be there for you." He smiled at her, dropping his forehead to hers and closing his eyes, breathing deeply.

"I know you will," she whispered back, her eyes fluttering closed as his arms wrapped around her. Time seemed to stand still as she sat with Gage, and she felt her worries slip away, at least for now.

Chapter 3

Time seemed to stand still as she sat with Gage, and she felt her worries slip away, at least for now. He made her believe in herself, and knew he would always be right beside her when she stumbled. He would prop her up when she felt weak and would stand back and bask in her successes. There was no one on earth she would rather have on her side than Gage. Her heart swelled.

She took a deep breath and raised her head. "Thank you."

"Always," he smiled.

Together, they walked hand in hand back to Suleima's cabin. Returning in time to watch Dynasira land, just outside of the wards around her home.

"I've sent scouts to see what they can find. We should bring what we do know to the council," Dynasira said, shifting into her human form. Her royal blue hair shining with each patch of sunlight she walked through.

"I agree," Gage said. "Others on the council may know of, or have other ideas on how to track down Sumar."

"Summon the council. We'll meet before the day is over. Hopefully, we will have more information to go on by the time we meet, but if not, I believe you are right. Maybe they'll have some insight into how to track Sumar down. Or even Kylin, if it comes down to it."

The sun was past its zenith as Suleima arrived at the warehouse the council was using for their meeting place. Only Dynasira was representing the dragons so far, but Gage and Kaly were present for the werewolves. Suleima was anxious for the arrival of Lysom and Xiala, the other two shamans on the council. She hoped they had some familiarity with Sumar or Kylin. They greeted each other before taking their places and awaiting the arrival of the remaining council members.

It didn't take long before all the members of the council were sitting around the table, anxiously awaiting why they were called.

"Thank you for coming this evening. The reason I have called this meeting is because I have identified the magical signature of the obsidian I found in Dirrin's tent," Suleima began. "The signature belongs to a long passed shaman I knew as a young girl. Her name was Kylin, and was trained by Sumar."

Lysom spoke up, "How is this possible?"

"I'm not sure. That is why I have called this meeting. Dyna has sent some scouts out to see if they can locate Sumar. I have also sent messages to several other shamans in hopes they will have some information. I'm also hoping you, Lysom and Xiala, will be able to help find some information from the shaman you are familiar with. Between the four of us, I'm confident we can make some progress."

"No one brings back shaman; we're useless once brought back using necromancy," Xiala said, furrowing her brow.

"Yes," Suleima replied. She looked around at the others seated at the table, explaining Xiala's comment, "Once a shaman passes, their powers return to the elements. If a necromancer would bring them back, it would be no different than bringing back a human. Our connection to the elements would not return with us.

"I don't understand how this may have happened. But, I'm certain it *is* her magical signature on the obsidian we found. There is no way there could be her magical signature would still be present nearly fourteen years after she passed. And, I know for a fact she passed before she had acquired skills and honed her talent enough to be able to channel her power to make something so complicated as a chunk of obsidian."

Lysom chimed in again, "I remember hearing about Sumar pulling away from mentoring. One of his other students went to work with a mentor who worked closely with mine. I'll see what I can find out."

"Thank you, Lysom." Suleima paused for a moment. "I have years of Erist's journals. I have only read the entries around the time of Kylin's passing so far. I'll continue to dig through his writings to see if there is any more information we can get from him."

Dynasira spoke up. "I should hear something by tomorrow from my scouts. I'll bring the information to you as soon as it comes in."

"My pack is ready and willing to help; you only need to call on us," Gage added.

"The jinn will keep our ears open for any rumblings which may be related. A lot of my kind are on the periphery, so I don't know what help we could be, but we'll be on alert just the same," Hamanad added.

"I appreciate it, Hamanad. I believe collectively we can get to the bottom of this. This is why the council was formed and this will be the first test of our abilities, our chance to show our community not only can we all work together cohesively as a team, but together we are stronger and together we can protect our world as a whole.

"I cannot explain this feeling... something comes our way, and only together can we find and vanquish this danger."

As the meeting wound to a close, Dynasira approached Suleima, where she stood with Gage and Kaly. "I'll return in the morning with news from the scouts. Do you want me to fly you home before I head out?"

"No, please go and rest. I'll make my way home," she replied.

Dynasira nodded, then headed out the door, shifting and taking flight, with Agron on her heels. The shaman and jinn followed close behind.

"What can the wolves do to help?" Kaly asked.

"For right now, stay alert."

"Will do. Gage, I'm going to head over to the pack house."

"OK, Kaly. I'll see you there later," he replied.

"You can go back with Kaly if you need. You don't need to babysit me."

"I have no intention of babysitting you, Sul. If I know you, you're going to go home and start combing through Erist's writings. Someone needs to make sure you take care of yourself in the process of taking care of the rest of us." He winked at her, then placed his hand on the small of her back, guiding her to her car, before tucking her into the passenger seat. "I'll see you home and help with whatever I can before coming back to the pack house."

Chapter 4

THE DRIVE TO THE cabin was quiet, Suleima concentrating on the task that lay ahead. Erist's writings were a painful reminder of him. She quietly wiped away a stray tear. Gage must have noticed, because he took her hand in his, lazily rubbing the back of her hand with his thumb.

She gave him a sad smile. He would be there for her in the tough moments. She squeezed his hand. Together, they would get through this.

Gage parked her truck, and they hiked the last mile to her cabin, the cool breeze through the shady trees keeping away the heat of the day. She checked her wards, finding them undisturbed before she and Gage entered her home. She gathered all Erist's journals from beneath her bed this time, not just those which covered the time of Kylin's passing.

The journals were leatherbound and smooth to the touch after years of use and care. She brought the books to the table and began reading when she and Erist first began to go meet with Sumar and Kylin. Suleima would have been around ten at the time. Just over a year after beginning her training. Erist wrote of her potential in his journals, saying plainly how proud he was of her and her earth affinity. He worried she was holding back some of her power and was not sure how to help Suleima tap into it, but there was also a hesitancy she didn't understand. She didn't remember Erist being hesitant to train her. To her, their time together was as natural as breathing.

It was bittersweet to see what was happening in Erist's mind. He wrote details she had forgotten until that moment. Things which would make her smile, things that would make her cry. And through all of it, Gage was there to support her. She read passages out loud to him. Like the first time he tried to teach her to use fire. Suleima was only able to get the wooden log to smolder. She was so disappointed in her performance. And Erist, trying to make her to understand it was just the beginning, tried to encourage her smolder to ignite into a small flame using his own magic. Suleima had given a final shove with her magic and, with the combination of Erist's and hers, blew the log apart, knocking Erist back on his behind, leaving him with a comical, ash covered face and his hair blown every which way. She had been terrified he would be upset with her, but Erist began to belly laugh, encouraging her to join in.

Gage laughed along with her, comforting her when the story ended with her in silent tears, missing her mentor and friend.

Not once, however, did Erist mention the location of Sumar and Kylin's home, or of any lake house belonging to Sumar. All this information, these stories, the training and there was nothing useful. She closed the latest book harder than she intended, startling Gage.

"What is the matter?" he asked.

"There's so much here, but nothing I am *looking* for!"

"Let's take a break. Go for a walk, clear your head. We can talk about what you've read or talk about nothing. You decide."

She nodded and rose from her chair, heading for the door. Suleima didn't venture far, content to sit on the porch, looking out into the woods beyond her house. Gage sat next to her, their legs touching, his arm behind her, sitting silently. After yawning, she laid her head on his shoulder. He tilted his head down to touch hers and held her hand.

They hadn't had time to define what was happening between the two of them. She knew she enjoyed his company and wanted to spend more time with him. But things had been so chaotic since the two of them met. Gage's friendship and strength were things she was beginning to rely on, and it was scary and wonderful at the same time. She thought he felt the same. It was usually Gage who initiated the first touch, and it had never gone beyond holding hands or sitting close. She certainly didn't want to jeopardize their friendship, and danger was never far in all of their time together, it seemed.

Suleima drifted off to sleep like that.

She was sitting in her house again, going over and over the journals lying on the table. There was nothing. Nothing. Nothing! What good was all of this journaling and documenting of EVERYTHING, if it wasn't going to be helpful to her situation?

Damnit, Erist!

Suddenly, she felt weightless and woke with a start. She was in Gage's arms as he jumped the railing of the porch and took off in a full sprint into the yard beyond. "What happened?" she cried out.

The growl in his voice raised the hairs on the back of her neck. "I don't know!" He set her on her feet and put himself between her and her home. "Don't move. I'm going to shift. Stay right here!"

"Gage, my wards...."

"Shtay heree!" Gage's words were a guttural growl and his elongating jaw distorted his words.

She shifted her weight, and his growl sounded again. "Okay, I'll wait for you." She raised her arms in surrender. "My wards are in place and intact. Whatever you heard is not a danger."

He growled once more, and she sensed him pulling from the pack to speed his shift.

Her next move was to sit and patiently wait him out.

A few minutes later, Gage shook out his fur and turned to her.

"Can I go now?" she asked.

Gage showed her his large, white fangs.

"I'm telling you, nothing got past my wards."

He grumbled next to her and kept his own body between her and her home, but he allowed her to follow.

Walking up to the porch, Suleima saw nothing out of the ordinary. She approached the door, but Gage put himself in the doorway and wouldn't move. Despite his grumblings, she leaned into the doorway above him to survey her home. Tea dripped from her ceiling onto the table and floor below. Her tea kettle seemed to have...exploded.

"What the...?" She again tried to push past Gage, but he was immovable. "I need to go in and clean up this mess. I don't sense anyone else in the area. But I do need to look and find out what happened."

He planted himself in the center of the doorway and refused to budge, sitting in the way as if he were bored.

"Fine!" She stomped her foot and sat on the railing of the house. "Go satisfy this neanderthal need to clear the house, while the little weakling woman sits on the porch and waits alone for the boogeyman to come while you are inside. And watch where you step. I don't want to clean blood off my floor as well." She waved her hand dismissively at him.

His tongue lolled out of his mouth as if he was smiling. He jumped to his feet and wandered happily into the cabin, sniffing all around.

Suleima followed him as far as the doorway of the house, respecting his wishes, but stood, tapping her foot impatiently, until he huffed indicating he was finished.

"Told you." She childishly stuck her tongue out at him, then went in and cleaned up the mess, while he went back outside to shift. While she waited, Suleima made a quick snack for him, knowing he would be hungry after two such rapid changes.

"What happened?" Gage asked, pulling his shirt over his head as he strolled back into the cabin.

"I don't know." Suleima handed him a plate and sat down heavily in her chair. "I sense only my magic in the house. And the teacup and kettle were nowhere near the stove, so excessive heat didn't cause them to burst. I don't have any clue what happened."

Gage ate his food, his eyes roaming the room periodically.

"The danger has passed, Gage. You can go off of high alert. Do you see any corners to hide in in this little cabin?"

"Not a chance. Something weird just happened. I don't know what or how, but until I have those answers, I don't think you should stay here."

"Ha. You're funny. Sorry. Not going to happen. I can protect my-self. And this is not your territory. You don't get to Alpha me around."

Gage sighed.

"I am perfectly capable of taking care of myself. Now, finish your plate of food. I'm going to continue to read in the journals."

Suleima opened yet another journal and began to read.

Somewhere in the back of her mind, she had hoped she would find some nugget of information which would tell her why Dirrin turned out the way he did. But at least through the end of the current journal, Erist was just as proud of the potential and progress of Dirrin as he was of Suleima.

In the next journal, there were fewer and fewer visits to train with Sumar and Kylin, because she was becoming more and more frail as her illness grabbed hold. Erist never mentioned what the illness was in his journals, and Suleima could not remember anyone ever mentioning it. Kylin had been a small girl to begin with and did not have the weight to lose; she was merely skin and bones. Her white-blonde hair reached nearly to her waist but had become thin and stringy. Her cheeks were sunken in, as well as her eyes, giving her a skeletal quality which scared Suleima at their last visit.

Closing the journal, Suleima stretched out her stiff muscles and yawned. "I'm going to call it a night with these journals. Did you want me to drive you back to the pack house?"

"What happened when we were outside? What caused the cup and kettle to burst?"

"I don't know."

"Until you know, you will have a houseguest." Gage walked out onto the porch, closing the door behind him.

Suleima shook her head, smiling, then set about replenishing her power stores and preparing for bed. She opened the door when Gage scratched at it, then climbed into bed after making sure her wards were in place. Gage curled up on the foot of the bed, his muzzle resting on his front paws and his eyes scanning the one-room cabin.

Chapter 5

Suleima awoke to soft growling. Gage sat at the door, his body alert and a low rumble emitting from his throat. Suleima reached out with her magic, then got up and placed a calming hand on his head. "It is just a messenger bird. Lysom must have found something. It carries his magic." She started to open the door, then paused. "Please stay inside. I would rather you not scare away the bird with the important message."

Gage huffed, backed away from the door, and sat again.

Suleima retrieved the message from the bird and came back inside, shaking her head. "It seems I'm taking another trip. Lysom has located Sumar at his lake house a few hours east of Setura. I'll be back in a few days."

Gage growled.

"You need to stay here with your pack. It won't be dangerous. And even if it were, I'm fully capable of defending myself."

Gage growled again and walked out onto the porch and into the forest beyond.

She was nearly finished packing when Gage reappeared. The look on his face as he approached the cabin showed how unhappy he was. "Before you start on me, I'm capable of going on a trip by myself. Also, I need you to stay here. You need to keep the pack going with the protection of the lands where Dirrin and his minions were camped out. This is also the base for the council. Since I won't be here, I need you to be."

"You need someone who will be able to back you up *if* you need it. I know you are capable of handling anything thrown at you, but I don't want anything to happen to you and you are *safer* if you have backup," Gage said.

"I'll be going with her," Dynasira piped in from the doorway.

"I don't need a babysitter," Suleima whined.

"I'm not a babysitter. We are going on a girls' trip, and who is going to search through Sumar's cabinets while you're distracting him, to find out all the things he doesn't want us to know?"

Suleima shook her head and completed her packing. Gage carried her bag out to her truck, while Suleima reinforced the wards on her home since she would be gone for several days.

She drove Gage back to the pack house while Dynasira flew above. Gage was quiet the entire journey, and she let him have his silence.

As she pulled into the driveway and parked the car, Gage turned to her. "I don't like that you are going without me. But I understand your reasons. I'm glad you are at least taking Dyna." He paused a moment before continuing, "You had better come back in one piece and unharmed." He planted a swift kiss on her lips, gave her a wolfish grin, leaped from the car and went into the house, leaving her stunned.

A moment later, Dynasira hopped into the seat Gage had just vacated. "I guess I am ready to ride in this death trap for the next few days." Then she added, "What did I miss?"

They had been driving for a while in silence, Suleima still in shock, when she suddenly said, "He kissed me."

"Ha!" she replied, "Finally!"

"He kissed me and then ran!" Suleima said.

"Wait, what?" Dynasira exclaimed.

"He kissed me and then jumped out of the car and ran to the house," she replied, "What am I supposed to do with that?"

"Well, first," Dynasira began, "We go and get this Sumar guy and figure out what the hell is going on. Then we go home and take turns smacking the Alpha around a bit. Then you kiss him."

"Wait, what?" Suleima echoed.

"You like him, right?" Dynasira said.

"Well yeah, but...," Suleima started.

"No buts. You like him. He likes you. See where this goes." Dynasira got a wistful look on her face. "Life is too short to worry about the what ifs..."

"I am so sorry," Suleima started. Dynasira still suffered from the loss of her fiancé.

"Nothing to be sorry for. Learn from my experience. He could be gone in an instant. Or you could. Cherish each and every moment you have with him." Dynasira finished.

"Thank you, my friend," Suleima added, before lapsing back into a silent ride, thinking about the events of the last few months and the time she was able to spend with Gage.

A few hours later, Suleima and Dynasira switched off. Dynasira hated to drive, but Suleima needed a break. As they headed down the road again, Suleima told Dynasira about the exploding kettle and cup from the night before.

"You only sensed your magic and nothing crossed your wards?" Dynasira inquired. At Suleima's nod, she continued, "What were you and Gage doing when it happened? Were you inside?"

"No, we were on the porch and I fell asleep against his shoulder."

Dynasira's smile could have lit up a room.

"Yeah, yeah... back to the kettle exploding."

"You said it was not near the stove, and you sensed no one else's magic." Dynasira clarified.

"Right, both were on the kitchen table and no, I couldn't find another magic signature."

"There has to be some explanation for it. Did you somehow use your magic to do it?"

"I was asleep!"

"And?" Dynasira replied.

"Again, I was asleep. I have to actually concentrate to cast a spell. And why would I break my kettle and cup?"

"I'm just trying to help," Dynasira said. "What did Gage think?

"He refused to let me into the cabin until he had cleared the place, even though my wards were intact, and the only magic was mine."

"I'll try to think on it some more. But my bet is it was triggered by your magic somehow."

"I don't know how that would even be possible, Dyna. Wielding magic takes concentration," she replied.

"We'll figure it out. Between you, Gage and I, we'll get to the bottom of what happened. It's a mystery for tomorrow. For now, we need to concentrate on how and what we're going to say to Sumar."

She hoped Sumar had not changed much over the years, but after years as a recluse, he was probably not going to be happy about having people standing on his doorstep.

Driving through Setura, Suleima kept her eyes on the road and tried not to look around. This place held so many memories, and the most recent ones were scary and sad. Involuntarily, she flexed her left hand. She still kept the glamor in place most of the time to hide her scars. This is where Dirrin had nearly won, where she had nearly lost her life, and was now irrevocably changed in so many ways.

Dynasira kept her eyes on the road as well. She had been beside Suleima during the battle. Dynasira had hidden her away, helped to nurse Suleima back to health, at least until Suleima was well enough to leave to continue her recovery in Amber Mountain. Dynasira had lost friends and family in that battle, and before, to Dirrin and his minions. The scars for both of them ran deep, and neither would ever be fully healed.

They stopped for the night a couple of hours away from Sumar's lake house, thinking it best to arrive earlier in the day. The night passed quickly and, they were back on the road as the sun peeked over the horizon.

Chapter 6

THEY PULLED INTO THE long lane leading to the lake house at mid-morning. Suleima pulled the truck off to the side of the lane after turning it around. "We'll leave the truck here and walk the rest of the way."

"Any particular reason?" Dynasira asked.

"Just a feeling. I can't explain it."

"I trust you. We can walk in. I can get us out in a hurry if necessary."

Suleima opened her senses, looking for anything that gave her pause. Wildlife moved about in the surrounding trees; nothing acting any different than she would expect. Suleima started forward, with Dynasira close on her heels. She continued to draw as much information from her surroundings as possible.

As the house came into view, she finally registered a very weak ward directly around the house. They approached slowly. The front of had a very small porch, only big enough for a small table and one chair. She could see the lake to the north of the home, and that side of the house had what looked to be a large deck which looked out on the gorgeous lake. From where they stood, no other buildings were visible. Forest surrounded the house on every other side.

When Suleima reached the stairs to the front porch, she motioned for Dynasira to stay back for a moment and dropped her glamor, extending her left arm. She sent a pulse of her magic into the ward, a shaman's way of knocking, replaced her glamor, and stepped back.

Sumar opened the door, and their eyes met. Suleima took a second step back involuntarily. Something was wrong. Dynasira tried to step to the side, but Suleima shot her arm, stopping the movement.

Keeping herself between Dynasira and Sumar, Suleima lowered her eyes. "Sumar, sir, I am Suleima, student of Erist. I have come to speak with you if you would allow it."

Sumar's eyes narrowed for a moment, then cleared. The ward pulsed, allowing her entrance. She took a step forward. Keeping Dynasira behind her, she cautiously approached the porch steps.

"It has been many years since Erist passed, and many years before since he last visited with a student, and never here," Sumar said.

Suleima was hesitant to share too much information until she knew what happened to Sumar and why she suddenly seemed so uneasy. "I had hoped to visit with you. There were such happy times coming to work with you and Kylin."

"And your backup?" he asked, motioning to Dynasira.

"She is my best friend. It was a long journey to travel here, knowing I would need to drive through Setura. It was a comfort having a friend along." Suleima replied easily.

Sumar seemed to dismiss Dynasira and turned. "Follow me to the back deck." His voice was almost robotic.

They followed him at a bit of a distance, walking through a very sparse living room and kitchen, exiting onto the deck from a sliding glass door that took up most of one wall of the kitchen. The sunlight glistened on the surface of the lake, blinding her to some of the surrounding forest. She reached out her senses. The lighting seemed wrong. Was it brighter out front, outside of the ward? But she noticed nothing out of the ordinary as she scanned the property.

She sat in the chair Sumar indicated. Dynasira stood behind her, leaning on the side rail, since there were only two chairs. Sumar sat across from Suleima, his attention a mystery.

They sat quietly for a moment, Suleima waiting for his attention to turn to her, but it did not seem like he would on his own.

"Sumar, how have you been these last years?" she asked.

"I have stayed here, alone and on my own," he responded. It could have been to be a trick of the light, but a strange cloud floated across his eyes.

"You have had no visitors since coming here?"

"I have stayed here, alone and on my own." That strange cloud reappeared and disappeared as quickly as before.

"Lately, I have thought of Kylin. Maybe just because I saw Dirrin recently, but it made me think of you, and gave me the idea to come visit."

He tilted his head strangely. "Dirrin was a fine student for a while. Kylin...." his voice trailed off.

"Forgive me Sumar, I was unable to come in person to offer my condolences at the time of Kylin's passing," Suleima said gently.

"Kylin was my best student." His voice was back to being robotic.

"Is there a place I could go to honor her? Lay flowers by her burial site, or someplace she held special?" Suleima asked softly.

"Kylin passed many years ago. She was my best student."

"I was so sad to have missed her celebration of life. I wish I could find some way to pay my respects and apologize," Suleima kept her voice low and rhythmic.

"Kylin passed away many years ago. She was my best student," Sumar repeated. "I have been here alone." His tone became impatient.

Dynasira stood straight up from her leaning position and placed a hand on Suleima's shoulder.

Suleima closed her eyes for a moment, seeing with her senses rather than her eyes. A cloud hovered over the lake house. She tried to pull at a thread of the spell she could now feel surrounding the house, but it refused to budge and, after a jolt to her hand, she let go. The magic she knew, and it was not Sumar's.

When she opened her eyes, Sumar was staring at her. "Why have you really come, Suleima?"

"Only to see an old friend. I apologize for disturbing your peace. If I had known another way to contact you, I would not have shown up unannounced. You have a beautiful home. I will not disturb you any longer." Suleima rose from her chair.

"*No!*" Sumar shouted, slamming his hand down onto the table. "Why did you come here?"

The ward solidified around the house with an audible snap.

Dynasira pulled at her throat, her eyes wild.

"Let her go, Sumar! She is no threat to you!" Suleima shouted, turning back to him. The magic she felt was his, but it was not only his. She tried pulling against the magic with her own, but it refused to release Dynasira. Suleima panicked. She tried to pull with her hands, but there was nothing to pull. The ward was a bubble encasing the house and deck, but not sinking into the ground at any point, preventing her from using the dirt and plants. Using air magic, she shoved Sumar to the ground, but it had no effect on the hold that was currently placed on Dynasira. She was on the verge of losing consciousness and Suleima needed to do *something*.

She screamed in frustration.

A jet of water pierced the ward as Dynasira sank to the ground.

Suleima scanned the forest with her senses. No one else approached. The ward shattered like glass. She could access the earth again. Vines grew quickly, winding around Sumar's arms and legs to keep him in place, and she grabbed Dynasira beneath both arms. Using her magic to help her, she pulled Dynasira onto the beach. Dynasira was breathing again, but unconscious all the same.

Suleima took a moment to give Dynasira a burst of healing energy. She kept a constant scan of the area surrounding her as she pulled Dynasira around the house. By the time they reached the front, Dynasira was able to stand, leaning on Suleima as they headed down the lane to the waiting truck.

As soon as Dynasira was in the truck, Suleima released the magic holding Sumar in place. She did one final scan of the area, started the engine, and pulled out as quickly as her old truck would go.

Dynasira was silent for the first few minutes of the trip then turned to Suleima. "What the hell happened back there?"

"I'm not sure. There is something over that house. Some cloud. It's not Sumar's magic. Or not *only* his magic. I couldn't find anyone else. But I felt Kylin's magic with Sumar's. That's impossible! But I felt her magic in that obsidian. Somehow, some way, she's still around, or at least her magic is, and someone is using it."

"Sumar was a robot. He kept repeating himself like he was programmed to read a script."

"Only a few creatures can do that."

"But you know of some?"

"A vampire," Suleima answered solemnly.

"Wait, what?" Dynasira looked at her as if she was crazy. "Vampires were eliminated long ago. And thank the elements for that! I cannot imagine what Dirrin would have been capable of with vampires at his side!"

"The *blood* vampires were eliminated almost a century ago. Energy vampires still exist. The fae created them. They feed off the energy and power of others to live. A side effect of feeding, they can cloud their prey's mind. I didn't realize they could control the being, but I've never really done much research on them because there were so few."

Suleima's heart was still pounding at the thought of the danger her friend had been in. "I'm eternally grateful for the spear of water you called. I couldn't break through the ward or the spell that was choking you."

"I didn't call any water spear. You know my magic doesn't work like that. I spit water in dragon form. I can't call it or manipulate it. Certainly not while looking human!"

"Then who..." Suleima trailed off. "I didn't sense anyone else."

"I think it was you, Sul."

"Me?"

"It certainly wasn't me. Sumar didn't create the spear. Certainly this energy vampire wouldn't have done it. It had to be you."

Suleima's brow furrowed in confusion. "I didn't pull on water. I used air to knock Sumar down."

Chapter 7

"WHERE ARE WE GOING?" Dynasira asked.

Suleima just shook her head. Tears threatened to stop her in her tracks. If she spoke or gave into those tears, she'd never make it to her destination. She took the road through town, then veered off onto a seldom driven path. Dynasira would recognize the route she was taking, if not why.

She smelled the smoke, long before the charred remains of Erist's home came into view. The fire was long extinguished, but the memory was so very fresh. The smell was all in her head. She parked the truck at the base of the porch, but just stared at the structure, not moving.

After a few moments, Dynasira asked, "Is there something I can go in and get for you?"

Suleima shook her head. After a few deep, steadying breaths, she said, "No. I need to go back in. Something is inside. Something still hidden. I'm not sure what it is or how I know it's there, but it's calling to me." She loosened and tightened her grip on the steering wheel several times, gathering her courage and determination before reaching for the door.

"Do you want me to stay here or come with you?"

"Please come too."

Dynasira stayed behind Suleima, allowing her to lead the way to whatever they were here for.

Suleima walked into the charred shell of the old hallway leading to the bedrooms. She stopped at the old door to her bedroom. The door was charred and scorched, and the patina of the knob was obviously from the intense heat of the blaze that claimed the only home she had known.

Dirrin's bedroom door was untouched by the flames, the symbol he'd burned into the door protecting it from the inferno. The pale birch was completely out of place in the blackened ruins of the rest of the house.

Erist's door was barely hanging on the hinges. Only a small section where the handle and center hinge was still intact and the knob was completely melted as if Dirrin had directed his fire to target anything of Erist's, though he had been long gone by the time the fire had spread this far. Suleima ducked under what was left of the door and went to the center of Erist's room. Everything inside was destroyed; ash was all that remained. The metal springs from the mattress, rusted from exposure, canted to the side.

Suleima closed her eyes to block out the sight and reached out with her senses. Whatever she was looking for was not in this room. She backed out the way she had come and returned to the hallway, back to her room, and tried the handle, but the mechanism inside must have melted and it would not turn. Dynasira pushed her to the side and kicked next to the door handle, breaking the brittle door, slamming into the wall inside her room.

Suleima nodded her thanks and entered the room. The fire failed to do the damage in here as it had in Erist's room. Everything was charred but still recognizable. Again, she closed her eyes and reached out. Whatever pulled her here to her old home wasn't in this room either.

She shuffled back down the hallway, trying to avoid the spongy spots. There was only one place left to look. Dirrin's room.

She picked her way back down the hall and placed her left hand on Dirrin's door. Any enchantment that he placed should have died with him, but she sent out a pulse of her magic to be sure. An echoing pulse answered her, but not from the door.

Suleima turned the knob and entered the room. It was completely untouched by Dirrin's fire. She had refused to look at, or enter, this room after Erist, after the fire. She closed her eyes and reached out again. The pulse drew her closer to the bed. Dynasira followed her into the room and stood on high alert, ready to shift at a moment's notice. Suleima held her magic at the ready.

She approached the bed and tried again, then tried pushing the bed away. Dynasira came to aid her, and together, they shoved the bed over to the wall.

Standing where the bed had been, Suleima reached out yet again. The boards under her feet pulsed back at her. She knelt and examined the boards closely. One board seemed slightly newer, with less wear and tear than the rest.

Suleima made her way to the kitchen and back, returning with an old, now rusted knife. It took several minutes of prying, but she finally lifted the board from its resting place enough that she saw a cloth wrapped around an object. She reached in and pulled it out. The weight and shape told her it was a book. She stood and reached out again with her magic, but nothing answered except for the pulse of the cloth-wrapped object in her arms. Suleima turned on her heels and headed back out to the truck, not stopping to look at any more of the surrounding destruction.

She climbed back into the driver's seat and placed the book on the bench between her and Dynasira.

"Don't you want to see what it is? Why you were drawn here?" Dynasira asked.

Suleima shook her head. "It is content now." She glanced down at the book. "It'll wait until we are away from here."

Suleima was determined to get home as quickly as possible. Suleima parked her truck in the usual spot, gathered her cloth-covered book and hiked back to her cabin, strengthening the wards before entering.

Suleima placed the book on her table and backed away from it.

"What's wrong now?" Dynasira asked.

"I'm not sure I want to read what's in that book. It must be important, or else it wouldn't have called to me. I'm just being cautious... or paranoid," she replied.

"It's late. Will it wait until tomorrow?"

"It'll have to. I'm not ready yet."

They said their goodbyes and Suleima fell into an exhausted sleep.

She sensed him the moment she awoke. Gage sat on her porch. She stretched and smiled before rolling out of bed and opening the door.

"Good morning," she said, peeking her head around the door frame. When their eyes met, she suddenly remembered how they parted and became shy.

Gage slid over a fraction and patted the spot next to him on the bench on the porch.

Suleima sat next to him, taking in the sounds of birds and smells of the forest surrounding them.

Gage took her hand in his and let out a sigh. "I'm glad you are home. And I'm glad you are okay. And I am *very* glad that you had Dyna with you." His grip tightened on her hand.

"You spoke with Dyna?"

"She came to the pack house to let me know you were home safe. Dyna was a little vague on details, but I got enough of the story to be happy she was with you."

"I was never in any danger; she was."

"And, if she hadn't been there, it might've been you that was in danger."

Suleima dropped her head to his shoulder and nodded. "I could have been, yes." She closed her eyes, breathing in his crisp, clean scent.

Gage shifted his body, wrapping her in his arms. When she sobbed suddenly, he pulled her into his lap and held her as she cried.

When the sobbing subsided, she pulled her head up. "I'm sorry."

He kissed her gently and then wiped her tears away, "No being sorry. You had a rough few days. I'm glad I can be here now."

He didn't run away this time after kissing her, but now she didn't know where to look or what to say. "I need to look at the book I found. Will you stay while I do?"

"Anything you need, Sul. Anything at all."

She forced herself to leave the safety and comfort of his arms and stood, walking to her open doorway. She paused, staring at the still covered book lying on her kitchen table. Gage placed his hand on the small of her back and she sighed, closing her eyes and taking a deep breath. She could do this. She had to do this. Taking one last deep breath, she forced her feet to move and walked to the table, sitting down hard, staring at the cloth covering the book.

Gage pulled the other chair over, almost touching hers, and sat down, their thighs brushing, and placed his arm over the back of her chair, tracing small circles on her upper arm with his thumb.

Suleima took a steadying breath and reached out. She examined the cloth. It was very dusty from being under a floorboard for who knew how long. But, until now, she hadn't noticed the quality of the fabric. Despite the silky feel of it between her fingers, the cloth was robust and durable. It held a warmth, like Erist's journals, a comforting heat to soothe her in moments of need. The fabric shimmered, iridescent despite the dust covering it. And something else, a familiarity, a feeling that she had seen and touched it before.

She folded the fabric gently, then placed it on her lap.

Turning her head, she met Gage's gaze. Her voice was small when she spoke, barely over a whisper, "I don't know what is in here. Do I want to know?"

Gage placed his hand on her cheek, never losing eye contact. "It will wait until you are ready." He shifted his hand, cradling her fingers within and stood, bringing her with him. "Let's take a walk."

Chapter 8

Suleima and Gage walked in silence through the trees of the forest surrounding Suleima's cabin. The song of nature buzzed around her. The chilly breeze raised goosebumps on her arm. Small animals scurried away as they approached, sensing the predator in their midst.

They entered a clearing with a crystal-clear lake. Gage led them to the shoreline and sat, pulling her down with him. When he finally spoke a few minutes later, it was in a whisper. "What keeps you from opening the book?"

She closed her eyes, tilting her head backward, soaking up the warmth of the sun. "Fear," she answered simply. "Erist's journals have always been special. It is my connection to him; the only connection I still have to him. He hid this one. My imagination is running wild with the possibilities of what could be in there."

"You said you felt it pulling for you. It's why you returned to his home."

"Yes." She thought a moment before continuing, "I've felt his pull before. In the end, it has always guided me in the right direction."

"But the right direction last time ended with us trekking up a mountain and facing dangerous creatures."

"I don't know if I am ready for another dose of that."

Dynasira landed behind them. "What did you find?"

"Nothing yet," Suleima answered. "I only took off the cloth covering it. The cloth alone is strange. I'm drawn to it. I can't explain it. When I had every intention of placing it on the table, I didn't. I put it on my lap. Opening it...."

Dynasira tilted her head thoughtfully before responding, "Let's ignore the book for now. We know that you sensed Kylin's magic on the obsidian and at Sumar's. Kylin's magic should have passed with her. And necromancy would not bring back her connection to the elements."

"Correct. But if she is an energy vampire now, which is the only explanation I can come up with, then she is a fae creation."

"How does that give her back her power over fire?" Gage asked. "You said she would lose any connection to her elements."

"Best guess? It's no longer a shamanistic connection to the elements. Fae magic, I believe uses the same elements, but their connection is different. We've severed the elemental connection to several of the shamans who fought with Dirrin. Their punishment is to live out the rest of their days as humans. That would never happen to fae. To be cut off from their magic is a death sentence."

<hr>

The next morning, Suleima absently braided her long hair as she thought about the upcoming council meeting. Right now, the evidence all pointed to Kylin and the fae. As much as she didn't want to believe it, no other explanation would fit. It had to be fae magic.

She gathered the journal and packed it carefully away. She placed a cloaking spell over it and the other journals to protect them should anything happen to her cabin.

Gage and Kaly were the first at the meeting. "What happened?" she asked.

"Someone snuck past my wolves last night at the campsite. They are two of my most reliable wolves. They both say they saw nothing, but something is off. My gut is screaming," Gage responded.

"Can you bring those wolves here now?" Suleima asked.

"I can be back here with them in ten minutes or so," Kaly said. She turned on her heel and headed out of the warehouse they used to meet.

"What do you think is happening?" Gage asked as Dynasira entered the meeting room.

"It's just a hunch. I promise I'll tell you more after I speak with your wolves." Suleima laid her hand on his forearm to reassure him.

Dynasira nodded. "You think it is the same as with Sumar?"

"That is my hunch."

By the time Kaly returned with the two shifters, the rest of the council had arrived.

Suleima called the meeting to order and asked Gage to report about the incident overnight.

"Someone breached Dirrin's tent. One chest is missing. As far as we know, there was nothing in the chest. It had been inspected by several shamans, including Suleima. So, we don't know why it was taken."

Lysom spoke up. "Kylin's body is not where it was laid to rest. There is no evidence anyone disturbed the spot recently."

Suleima took a deep breath and called over the wolves. As they spoke about the night before, a cloud passed over their eyes. The cloud was subtle but present, and the stories became identical, even though they'd positioned themselves in two different areas of the campsite. She asked each of them questions, in a couple of different ways, but their answers remained exactly the same, word for word.

Suleima dismissed them to their seats and addressed the council. "When Dynasira and I went to the lake house, Sumar reacted in much the same way. He had the same clouds pass over his eyes. Someone has tampered with their memories."

"How is that even possible?" Hamanad asked.

"The only explanation I can come up with is vampires."

Everyone began speaking at once. Suleima raised her hands to silence everyone. "Energy vampires can manipulate memories."

"The fae are not to be messed with," Hamanad said. "They are a dangerous lot, and getting tangled up with them could kill us all."

"We can't bury our heads in the sand and pretend none of this is happening, just because we suspect the fae might be involved. The entire purpose of this council is forfeit if we don't discover the truth behind these threats and do something about it," Suleima replied.

"My pack is behind you. No one messes with the memories of my wolves. I consider that a declaration of war." Gage pounded a fist on the table. "Whatever this threat and however we need to fight it, my wolves will be there."

Dynasira stood. "Dragons and fae have long avoided conflict with one another, knowing we are evenly matched and there would be great casualties on both sides. If they are threatening others and no longer remaining to themselves, then the dragons will stand against them."

Suleima held up her hands. "We aren't ready to go to war. We aren't even ready for another battle. Discovering what is going on needs to be our first priority. I won't target all the fae unless we learn they are moving as a whole. According to the stories, they don't get along with each other, let alone work together as one united front." She paused a moment before continuing, "Is there anyone here who knows or is familiar with any fae?"

The dragons and wolves shook their heads. Hamanad crossed his arms over his chest, before turning his nose up at the hint he would lower himself to befriend a fae. Lysom shook his head next.

Xiala spoke up, "I came across a fae years ago. He is a lesser fae, a barbegazi. He said he met a shaman long ago who was nice to him, so he came to me for aid when a fellow barbegazi needed healing. They have a passive magic which helps when there are avalanches, a warning system of some sort. They have no active magic, especially for healing. I have seen him occasionally when I have been out in the mountains since. He seemed friendly enough."

"Can you take me to him?" Suleima asked her.

"I can take you where I have normally found him. But, unless he wants to show himself, he won't," Xiala replied.

"You aren't going alone," Dynasira said emphatically.

"Xiala will be there," Suleima replied.

"So will I," Gage added. Suleima turned sharply to look at him. "No arguments this time. I'm coming along, even if I have to follow your scent."

Chapter 9

Over the next few hours, Suleima followed Xiala's directions, through the mountains. They followed a maintenance road for several miles before she told Suleima to pull off and turn off the engine. It was almost full dark.

"It's too late to start on foot tonight, but we should be on our way at first light," Xiala said. "The barbegazi are often out in the early morning. He loves honey, and I've harvested some fresh honey from near my home and mixed it into some treats."

"Gage and I can stay back a bit to allow you some space."

They lapsed into silence as they set up the tent in the bed of Suleima's truck so they were off of the cold hard ground. They snacked a little before bundling up for the night, Xiala in her blankets and Suleima in the sleeping bag she had taken to Mt. Lucent. Gage curled up with Suleima, sharing his body heat.

As dawn approached, they packed up their supplies, starting the trek up the mountain. Xiala led the way, and as promised, Suleima and Gage stayed back, keeping Xiala in sight.

About an hour into their trek, Xiala stopped and reached into her pack to pull out some of the treats.

At the edge of the wood stood a very small creature, probably less than two feet tall, with what looked like icicles hanging from his face. He was covered in white fur from head to ankle, with his feet strangely bare.

Gage bumped into Suleima's hip, his large teeth visible in a silent growl. Suleima knelt next to him, burying her hand in his ruff, holding him in place.

Suleima waited quietly. The gnome-like figure looked around for any sign of danger before leaving the tree line and heading over to Xiala. Xiala handed him some of the honey treats. Suleima cautiously stood, and keeping Gage behind her, slowly closed the distance between them and the gnome-like creature.

The closer she got to him, the wider his eyes seemed to grow. Up close, the barbegazi's eyes appeared almost white. Its skin resembled ice covered by a dusting of snow. Deep cracks surrounded its eyes like fissures in a glacier. The slight breeze, though it blew loose strands of her hair around her face, barely disturbed the icicle-like hair on the creature in front of her.

When she was a few feet away, she stopped and stooped to his eye level. "My name is..." she began.

"Suleima," he finished. His voice was deep for a creature so small.

"Yes. You know me?" she asked, her brows furrowing. The barbegazi nodded, then held his arms as if cradling a baby. Suleima sat back as he started talking quickly in a garbled and choppy language. More surprising than his recognition of her was the fact that she *understood* what he was chattering on quickly about.

"You should not have returned, young one."

Suleima heard Gage's soft growl but held her arm out behind her to stop him. The barbegazi placed his hand lightly on her cheek.

"Mama perished," came the gravely and stilted voice. "So sad. So lonely."

"I need to find a fae. Someone who would help me."

"No. Danger," the barbegazi said, forcefully.

"More danger if I do not. Something is happening. Something is coming. I need more information."

He looked from her to Gage, to Xiala, and back to her. "Alone," the barbegazi said reluctantly.

Gage's deep growl was not soft, now.

"Just the wolf and I," Suleima tried, "He comes too."

The barbegazi hesitated but dipped his head in affirmation.

Suleima turned to Xiala. "Head down to the truck. We will be back as soon as we can. If we don't return by sunrise, head back to Amber Mountain without us. Tell Dynasira where we went."

"What is going on?" Xiala asked.

Suleima adjusted her supply pack as she stood. "We will fill you in later."

Xiala narrowed her eyes, but turned on her heels in a huff and headed back the way they had come. Suleima nodded at the barbegazi and followed him back into the forest.

As they started up a mountain path, Suleima tried asking questions, but he would only respond by shaking his head. After several unsuccessful attempts to engage him, she went silent.

Chapter 10

After an hour of walking through the forest in what seemed like circles, they came to a small home. Warm light shone through the two windows in front. The cottage face was built into the side of a rocky outcropping. Suleima could sense the ward surrounding it and did not dare approach. The power she sensed in the ward was intense. The barbegazi pointed at her feet, which she took as a signal to stay there. He walked through the ward, approaching the door. He knocked and waited.

Gage pushed her behind him, but Suleima placed her hand on the fur at his neck, holding him in place. If he charged the ward surrounding the home, he would be killed. Her skin tingled with the menace behind the power.

The door opened. An ethereal-looking woman with white-blonde hair stood at the door, looking directly at Suleima with eyes which were the palest blue, almost white. Her gown matched her eyes and shimmered as it caught the rays of light peeking through the trees. The woman's eyes narrowed at her but softened when she looked at the barbegazi, who was speaking animatedly.

She gave a slight nod, and the barbegazi turned to Suleima, running to her side and grabbing her hand to pull her along. Gage let his disapproval be known. He snarled and snapped his jaws.

"Peace, wolf," came the musical voice of the woman standing in the doorway in front of them. "No harm to either of you, so long as you are in my home."

Suleima sensed the ward drop, though the woman made no physical movements. She took a step forward, keeping her hand in Gage's fur. Slowly, she followed the barbegazi to the door of the house.

The woman turned, leading the way into a large sitting room which never should have fit in the house she could see from outside. The door closed with a loud bang behind her, making her jump and Gage growl.

The barbegazi motioned for Suleima to sit in a chair directly across from the woman. Suleima placed her bow on the floor next to her chair. Gage sat directly in front of her, pressed tightly to her legs.

The room was opulent. A large chandelier hung from the vaulted ceiling, the light seeming to change color as it passed through the iridescent crystals enveloping the entire structure. The walls and ceiling were a soft white with dark wooden beams spanning the length of the ceiling. Dark wood floors matched the wooden beams of the ceiling but had mostly been covered in lush rugs in hues of blue. The woman sat in a chair reminiscent of a throne, high-backed with royal blue fabric covering it. Wooden accents on the chair were adorned with gemstones in every shade of blue. A large bay window, which should have been covered by the rocky cliff the house was built into, showed a view of a lovely snow-covered meadow with an ice-covered lake in the center.

The woman smiled softly at Suleima, waiting for her to speak. "My name is Suleima," she started.

"I know who you are, child," the woman interrupted. "Why have you come here?"

"I have suspicions there is a fae involved in a dangerous plot," she answered, adding, "What should I call you? And how do you know me?"

"The questions about you, I can answer. The questions about other fae, I do not know," she replied. "As for me, you may call me Zenisa. I rule here as the Ice Goddess."

"When did we meet?" Suleima asked.

"We have never met. But I am very familiar with you, young one."

She didn't even try to hide her confusion.

"You were just a small child when you left with the shaman." The statement from the barbegazi was spoken in his language, but she understood him clearly.

Understanding him should be impossible. She never encountered fae before or was taught their language. "The spell cast on you is to remove your memories. Your knowledge of the language you used as a child is still intact." Zenisa shrugged her shoulders dismissively.

"Wait!" Suleima held her hand up. "I'm under a spell? How? Why?"

"Vorelar helped your mother until her death. He would be better equipped to provide you with the details you seek." Zenisa indicated the barbegazi. Since they entered the room, his eyes never strayed from her.

Vorelar approached her slowly, his hand extended. Gage bared his teeth and a low growl rumbled through as the barbegazi walked closer. He chattered quickly in his native tongue.

She spoke to Vorelar, asking him to wait for a moment, then placed her hand on Gage's neck to catch his attention. "He needs to touch me. He can show me what happened. Vorelar says seeing is better."

The barbegazi closed the distance between them, stopping close enough to touch her face. He asked her to close her eyes.

Suleima kept her hand tangled in Gage's fur to keep him calm and center herself. She took a deep breath to calm herself and then closed her eyes. A brief sensation of falling overtook her before her stomach settled. Her fingers, still buried in Gage's soft fur told her she was still sitting on the chair inside the Ice Goddess's home, but the vision in her mind told her she sat outside on a snowy mountain, the wind whipping and howling around her in a wicked storm. Casting her eyes downward, she saw the legs of the Vorelar in front of her, one leg twisted at an unnatural angle. She herself made no sound but felt the vibration of a whimper in her throat, the sound made only in the vision she was immersed in. She realized she was seeing this vision literally from Vorelar's eyes, as it had happened.

A shadow appeared in the wall of snow in front of her and she experienced intense fear as the good leg of Vorelar worked along with his arms, trying to back away from the advancing shadow. The image towered over her as it continued to get closer and closer. Her heart pounded in time with the barbegazi's.

Despite Vorelar's continued fear, Suleima was able to calm her own racing heart at the sight of her beloved mentor, Erist, emerging from the wall of snow.

Erist towered over her as the barbegazi, but he carefully knelt and used a calm tone to soothe the frightened Vorelar. After examining him, Erist walked a few feet away to get a stick and splinted the barbegazi's leg. Next, Erist built a small fire and shared his rations with Vorelar, staying beside him through the night.

The next morning, feeling much improved, the barbegazi began chattering at Erist. Standing, with the help of Erist, Vorelar motioned wildly with his hands, trying to get the shaman to follow him. Despite his injury and using a stick as a crutch, Vorelar buzzed through the snow, checking back to make sure Erist was following him.

After about an hour, a small cottage came into view. Cheerful light spilled from the windows while snow covered the roof and piled against the wall of the house, obscuring the color. Vorelar's hand lifted and knocked on the door before backing up and waiting. Footsteps sounded and the door opened. The woman was tall and slender with her long, auburn hair wound into a complicated plait. She kept shifting her violet eyes from Vorelar to Erist and back again. Her posture was stiff, and Suleima could feel the magic the woman held close as she eyed the strange man standing just off her porch. She backed away from the door as if frightened, not in invitation, and began animatedly speaking with the barbegazi in the strange language.

After completing their long conversation, the woman looked warily at Erist, before inviting him into the cabin. She brought him a cup of hot tea to warm him. The barbegazi continued to speak animatedly. Periodically, she would emphatically shake her head no but otherwise did not speak.

The woman was a high-fae, like the Ice Goddess, human in stature and very powerful. Suddenly, the woman's eyes grew wide and concerned. Vorelar turned and Suleima spotted a young girl with auburn hair, just slightly darker than the fae woman's. The girl's eyes were gray, almost silver, and they widened in fear when the fae woman shouted and pulled a ball of ice from thin air to launch at Erist.

The little girl ran into the kitchen.

Suleima felt the barbegazi's shock as Erist pulled an air shield in front of him. In the same movement, he pulled the young girl behind him, protecting her with his body.

The woman's eyes widened, and the ball of ice dissipated. "You would shield this child you do not know with your own body, knowing my power would destroy you?" she said incredulously.

"This child is an innocent. She did nothing to incur your wrath," he responded, dropping his air shield. The moment his shield fell, the young girl conjured her own air shield. Erist stared at the young child. "She is of the elements. A shaman."

The woman stepped forward, her arms raised in surrender. "She is. She is also fae." The woman sat down at the table and called the young girl to her. "Her father was a shaman. He was killed many years ago for his love of a fae woman. I have kept her hidden away, but her shamanistic powers are beginning to manifest. She shows no affinity for fae powers. Her father had an affinity for air. I feel her strength in earth. If the fae find her here, she will suffer the same fate as her father."

"I am not a mentor. Teaching was never my intention. I have no experience with children," Erist told her.

"I have seen your kindness. You helped my friend, a fae, who you did not know. You protected my child, knowing I could destroy you. She needs to learn to harness her powers. I cannot teach her the ways of shaman. And I am dying. The goddess whispers to me that you will protect my child, teach her. You will help my child to thrive. She never needs to have knowledge of me. She never needs to know of her fae side. Those powers have not manifested in her. She would be shunned by both shaman and fae knowing her bloodline. I can make her forget," she continued. A single tear ran down the woman's cheek. "Please keep my young one safe. Teach her to protect herself. I see a bright future for my child, but only if she is far from here."

Before Erist responded, the woman whispered into the young girl's ear and kissed her on the forehead. The child dropped to the ground. Erist barely reached her before she hit the floor. When he looked up, the woman was gone.

Her vision shifted as Vorelar went into another room, a child's bedroom, and picked up a bag made of fine cloth. It was the cloth she had only just held a day ago. After placing some clothes inside, the barbegazi set a note gently on top—Suleima's name in a loopy script--and carried it back into the kitchen, where Erist remained, stunned, holding the sleeping child... the child was her. Vorelar handed the bag to Erist.

Suleima's stomach flip-flopped again and suddenly, she was back in the room with Gage and Zenisa. Vorelar had taken a step back, a single tear trailing down his cheek.

She reached into the pack sitting beside Gage on the floor and pulled out the bag she had seen in the vision, the bag which Erist had wrapped around his journal.

Raising her eyes to Zenisa, Suleima asked, "I am half fae?"

At her words, she felt Gage stiffen an instant in surprise, but he quickly leaned back into her leg, supporting her.

At the woman's nod of affirmation, she continued, "Why am I still alive?"

"I saw you were no threat to the fae. Your power is in the shaman side of you..." Her voice trailed off. She tilted her head, and a spark shone in her eyes, "Ahh, now I see. A late bloomer, I would guess. I sense the awakening of your fae magic."

Gage's body tensed beside her, preparing to defend Suleima violently.

"Easy, Alpha Wolf," the fae woman said. "She is still no threat to me or mine. Her future has not changed." She redirected her attention to

Suleima. "A water affinity. Different from your mother, but a compliment to your Earth magic. You have come here to ask for guidance in harnessing your fae power?"

"Until this moment, I had no knowledge of fae in my history. I came here to ask about a fae who might be threatening to follow the plans of a shaman to subjugate all of humanity and supernaturals."

Suleima paused, collecting her thoughts. "A water affinity? I was frustrated in my sleep and a tea kettle and cup in my kitchen shattered. A friend was in danger and I was blocked from using my shamanistic magic. A spear of water broke through the spell, which kept me from accessing the elements. I didn't consciously do anything. But if I am fae, was it me?"

"Our children often develop in much the same way, although their magic usually begins to manifest around the age of five or six at the latest," she said kindly. "In time, it will come easier to you. You can learn to guide the fae magic inside you. Right now, your magic flows to you when you least expect it, but most need it." The fae woman's head tilted and her brow furrowed. "You have touched Aether. How curious. I wonder if that was the catalyst to unlocking your fae magic."

"How did you...?"

Zenisa interrupted, "My secrets are my own."

There was no threat or malice in her voice, but Gage alerted just the same. He nearly vibrated where he sat, pressed tightly to Suleima's legs. Suleima nodded and waited for her to continue.

"You said you believe the fae are involved in something which poses a danger to the world. What makes you think the fae would even bother with mere humans?" Zenisa asked.

Sulemia carefully chose her words, reluctant to do or say anything which could offend the Ice Goddess. "I have encountered three people whose minds have been tampered with, their memories erased or altered. I believe it is the work of an energy vampire. I have also encountered the magic signature of a long dead shaman. Her body is missing from her original resting place. Necromancy with shaman is useless. They come back with no connection to the elements; they are no more powerful than an ordinary human."

"But brought back by a fae, as a vampire, their connection to the elements of the fae can be unlocked, assuming they can siphon enough energy from others to power themselves," Zenisa finished for her.

Suleima nodded.

"Those in my line, under my rule, do not have the ability to create vampires of any kind, nor would they be granted my permission. What was the affinity of this long dead shaman?" she asked.

"Kylin had an affinity for Fire," Suleima answered.

"Fire means the Sun Goddess and those she rules. They live far to the south of here. I would not advise you seek her council or ask her any questions. Although your fae magic is far underdeveloped, I can sense it on you now. She will as well. I fear you would not survive an encounter with her. Even with your brave Alpha wolf to protect you."

Gage bared his teeth again.

"Solisa has the knowledge and, I believe, would not hesitate to create an energy vampire, if she believed she would benefit from it," Zenisa continued, unconcerned with Gage's aggravation.

"Is there any way for me to reverse the altering of the memories?" she asked.

"Not at your current power level, and the longer the memories are altered, the more difficult it becomes," Zenisa answered. "You are untrained and your abilities are erratic. I feel them pulse even now."

"How can I learn more about my fae magic?"

"Ahh, that is the question. Do we want you to learn?" There was a warning glint in her eyes.

Gage's near-silent snarl became an intense growl.

"Hush wolf!" Zenisa warned before Suleima sensed magic settle over him.

She jumped to her feet and reached for the magic holding him. Her magic slid right off of whatever Zenisa had done with no effect. In a lightning-fast move, Suleima grabbed her bow from the floor and held an arrow, the bow string pulled tight.

Zenisa laughed at the display until Suleima fired her arrow, purposely missing Zenisa, but only by a hairsbreadth, a new arrow in place in the blink of an eye. "Release him. The next arrow will not miss."

Zenisa sobered. "You dare threaten me?"

"We came to you for help. Provide it, or tell us no, and we will be gone. We had no intention of threatening you, but we will defend ourselves from you if you make it necessary." Suleima dropped her bow slightly, "I said, release him. Now." She barely kept the threat from her voice. "Release him and we will go."

Zenisa seemed almost amused as the spell slid from Gage. Without a word, Suleima stepped forward and turned, walking to the door which would lead them back out onto the mountain.

Chapter 11

It was nearing dark when they left Zenisa's home.

"I don't know how much you got from the conversation..."

Gage nudged her when she didn't continue.

"I have no memory from before I came to Erist. I never have... still don't." She shook her head, then told Gage the story from the vision Vorelar shared with her.

Obviously, in wolf form, his ability to communicate was lacking, but he seemed to accept the news. She worried how the council would react. They continued down the path in silence for a while, Suleima lost in thought, trying to piece together everything she learned. If the Sun Goddess brought Kylin back, how and why? Why make her a vampire? What was her end goal? How long ago did she do it? Why go after Dirrin's books? Would the Sun Goddess's goal be similar to Dirrin's? Was the Sun Goddess even in charge of Kylin now that she was a vampire, or was the whole plan Kylin's?

Gage abruptly stopped and bared his teeth. Suleima laid a hand on his ruff and reached out with her senses. There was something out in the woods beyond her vision. It was tiny, barely a flicker in her senses. It seemed to flit from tree to tree, staying well hidden from view, especially in the waning light.

It bounced from tree to tree, slowly making its way closer. Suleima bent down to whisper in his ear, "I need to see what this is about. Please don't frighten it away." Although still baring his teeth, Gage at least stopped growling.

Making as little movement as possible, Suleima pulled at her power over air, forming a shield around herself and Gage.

It was just a few trees away now. The tension nearly poured from Gage in waves.

As it moved to the closest tree, Suleima saw what the creature was--a pixie. The tiny creature seemed to give off its own light source. It had a sparkle to it and was a shade of light green which allowed it to blend in with the foliage and light around the forest. Its iridescent wings fluttered quickly, like a hummingbird's wings, allowing it to dart quickly from one place to the next. It fluttered in their direction, stopping a hairsbreadth from the shield. It stuck out a tiny finger, and Suleima startled as the shield popped like a balloon and dissipated as if it had never been, followed by a tinny giggle.

Suleima tightened her hold on Gage's ruff as the pixie invaded the space her shield had protected. The pixie floated in front of her nose. It held out its hand, palm up, and pointed to Suleima.

Suleima copied the movement and the pixie landed on Suleima's hand, sitting cross-legged in the center of her palm.

"Whew!" she said in a high-pitched voice Suleima was surprised she could hear. "That was a trek. You move fast!"

Suleima eyed the pixie warily. "You were trying to catch up with us? Why?"

"I am Zia," she said, saluting Suleima, "Zenisa sent me. She believes I can help you unlock some of your fae magic. As well as provide you some insight when it comes to fae and their ways and habits." The pixie tilted her head, analyzing Suleima before speaking again. "You have a great strength in earth magic. Your connection to it calls to me. It is very strong, similar to my own. But I see what Mistress Zenisa was talking about. You have fae magic as well." The pixie rubbed her little hands together. "This is going to be fun!"

The pixie jumped off of Suleima's hand, her wings beating furiously as she slowly dropped to land on the end of Gage's snout. "Ooh, a puppy!"

Gage growled and snapped his teeth, barely missing the pixie as she flew just out of his reach.

"Grumpy puppy," Zia said.

"Please do not antagonize the Alpha Wolf," Suleima told the pixie as it landed on her shoulder, "He does not appreciate it, and neither do I."

The pixie nodded seriously. "Understood." She saluted Gage and turned, saluting Suleima, then began bouncing on the balls of her tiny feet. "Where to next? I have never been off the mountain!"

"First, we go to the truck, then we return to Amber Mountain," Suleima explained as they started walking again, the pixie parked comfortably on Suleima's shoulder and incessantly talked, asking questions about anything and everything.

When they were just out of sight of the truck, Gage stopped. She knelt down to his level, looking around to see what made him stop.

He bumped her with his snout and looked pointedly at the fae on her shoulder.

"You want me to leave her here?"

Gage huffed.

Kaly was usually there to help translate when she was speaking to Gage in wolf form. He pulled slightly on his own magic, then stopped.

Understanding dawned. "You want me to go get your change of clothes?" she asked.

Gage's tongue lolled out of his mouth in a smile.

"Okay. You wait here with Zia. I'll be back in just a minute." Suleima pulled Zia off of her shoulder and set her down on a fallen log a foot away from Gage. "You stay here with Gage. I will be right back."

Suleima walked down to the truck, impressed she only tripped once without Gage to guide her. Xiala sat on the tailgate of the truck.

"Any answers?" she asked as Suleima approached. "Bring along any friends?"

Suleima paused at the hostile tone. "Yes, we have a fae with us. And we'll fill you in, I promise. But right now, I need Gage's clothes so he can shift, and then we can rest before heading back to Amber Mountain." Suleima grabbed the change of clothes for Gage and turned to go back into the woods, where she left him. She paused before stepping out of sight. "For someone who made friends with a barbegazi, I am disappointed you would be upset at the sight of a fae." She turned sharply back to the trail and headed up to where she had left Gage and Zia.

Suleima laid Gage's clothes behind a nearby tree and left him there to shift, while she sat on the log next to Zia, while they waited.

When Gage emerged from behind the tree, he walked straight to Suleima, taking her hand and helping her to her feet. He did not release her hand as they headed back to the truck where Xiala waited, keeping her steady on the dark path. "I could hear the conversation when you returned to the truck. Xiala may be uncomfortable with the fae so close. If we need to drive out tonight, I'm able to do it."

"I would prefer to leave in the light. But thank you. We'll keep our options open."

Xiala had made her bed inside the cab.

The pixie flitted onto the bed of the truck, making herself a small bed on the top of the wheel well from some leaves from the ground.

Suleima buried her fingers into the loose dirt near the truck, placing a ward for the night.

It wasn't long after Gage lay next to her, that Suleima drifted off into a peaceful sleep, knowing she was protected by her wards, and by her wolf.

Chapter 12

In the truck the next morning, Xiala sat stiffly next to Gage, who remained in human form. Zia sat meekly on Suleima's shoulder on the side closest to the window. They only drove about fifteen minutes when Suleima abruptly pulled the truck to the side of the road.

"Out. Now." Suleima opened her door and climbed out, walking to the tailgate of the truck and leaning her hip against the back, her arms crossed.

Gage was next to her in moments. Xiala took her good old time.

"I will not drive the entire way to Amber Mountain in this uncomfortable silence. Xiala, what is the problem?" Suleima said, her tone agitated.

"What do you mean?"

"Do *not* play stupid. You know exactly what I mean."

"Why are we taking a fae to Amber Mountain?" Xiala asked.

"Because it's necessary. There is a better than good possibility the person who stole Dirrin's books is someone either fae or someone who is working for or has been brought back by the fae."

"That is even *more* reason not to have a fae with us!" she shouted.

"But you had no problem with a barbegazi?" Suleima asked.

"The barbegazi is *not* coming with us. The barbegazi is a lesser fae with no ties to fae with more power!" Xiala shouted. "You don't know anything about this sprite!"

"I am a pixie! Not a sprite!" Zia yelled back, stomping her foot on the truck's tailgate.

Xiala gave Zia a dismissive wave.

"Do you know who the barbegazi took us to?" Suleima asked Xiala. "The Ice Goddess. The most powerful fae on that mountain." Xiala's eyes widened. "The other reasons for bringing a fae with us will have to wait. It is a matter for the entire council. I expect you will be courteous for the remainder of the ride to Amber Mountain. Or I will make arrangements for you to be picked up here later, but you will *not* continue to treat this fae with disrespect and disdain. I will not have it. Make your decision."

"What would I do in the meantime?"

"Preferably, figure out how to work with others. You are no better than this pixie, and she is no better than you. If you judge her based on what she is, there is no place for you on this council." Suleima stated matter of factly. "I will make this known to the council and request a vote to remove you."

"I belong on this council!"

Gage placed himself between Suleima and Xiala, "If your idea of our council is not to work with us all equally, to keep peace among us, as well as between us and humans, you do not belong on it." His eyes narrowed and his body tightened. "I feel the magic you are gathering. If you intend to use it, you better hope it incapacitates me."

The menace in his voice brought chills to Suleima's skin. She pulled an air shield up in front of her and surrounding Gage and Zia, to keep him in place, for now. "Xiala, I hereby suspend you from your position on the council until a full vote can be made. Using your powers against another council member is strictly forbidden. Return your spell to the elements. This is the only warning you will receive."

"You are the one bringing in the fae!" Xiala's strength in air broke right through Suleima's own shield, shoving her backward into the shield she had erected around Gage. She heard his half howl, half shout as her back slammed hard enough to bruise. Luckily, Xiala's power was not enough to break through Gage's shield.

Suleima did not speak. She simply pulled. Her earth magic responded eagerly. She gave a burst of air, blowing the dirt below Xiala's feet into her eyes, breaking her focus and allowing Suleima to push against the air magic coming at her.

Xiala doubled her efforts, sending her wind to knock off tree branches from nearby trees and throw them in Suleima's direction. Using her own air, she sent bursts of air to knock the branches off course, mostly. She got hit by a few glancing blows.

Gage's rage increased. He was finished shifting, pawing at the dirt, trying to escape the shield trapping him. He released a frustrated howl.

Suleima understood his frustration. This was going nowhere. She didn't want to hurt Xiala, but to save Gage and Zia, she may not have a choice. She wanted to howl in frustration. Then it shimmered, that spark deep down, and she reached for it. It felt cool and fluid.

As soon as she felt it, it was gone. She tried grasping for it, but only lost her focus and got hit by yet another branch, knocking her to the ground.

Gage let one last howl rip before lunging through the shield. As he powered through, Suleima could smell the singed fur in the air. She dropped the shield quickly. He powered through Xiala's winds and dodged a few branches, the ones hitting him not even slowing him down. Xiala hit him with fire, knocking him back, using her wind to slam him into the ground. He let out a whimper.

Gage didn't make a sound when fighting. For him to make that whimper, to show any weakness, he was really hurt. Suleima let out a scream of frustration. A burst of water quickly became a wave. She surprised even herself with it, but she wasn't going to question it. It must be the fae magic. The wave hit Xiala, knocking her to the ground. Wave after wave kept Xiala on the ground, unable to regain her footing or gather her focus.

Suleima finally stood but continued her onslaught. She walked to where Xiala was pinned and gathered her earth magic, calling forth vines to tie her in place. She called away her voice as an extra precaution, turned on her heel, and headed to where Gage still lay, panting hard.

"Broken ribs," said Zia, fluttering just above Gage. "But you are powerful. Your mix of magics will be tough to master, but once you do, you will be hard to beat. You already do well with water. The waves were impressive. Your shamanistic magic and fae magic fight each other for dominance right now."

Suleima nodded, hearing what she was saying, but more concerned about Gage than her own magic right then. She lay a hand along his jaw. "You should have stayed back."

"A wolf protects its mate," Zia said.

Gage turned his head sharply and growled in her direction.

"Shh," Suleima said, drawing his attention back to her, "You'll hurt yourself more. Stay still." She leaned down touching her forehead to his. She closed her eyes and breathed deep to calm her own raging pulse. Seeing him in danger, again, sparked her own fierce protectiveness.

Clearing her mind of everything, she sent the little healing magic she knew into him. She felt him relax in relief. Pain was the only thing she could help with. He was a shifter, so he would heal quickly, but at least she could ease his pain a bit. His panting slowed.

"Should you shift?" she asked. His head moved slightly to the side, which she took to mean no. "Can you climb back into the truck?"

He very gingerly stood and limped in the direction of the truck.

Suleima jogged ahead and opened the passenger door, waiting until he got himself situated. She touched her forehead to his, giving a little more pain relief, then closed him inside, despite his growl when she did. The window in the truck was open. She directed Zia to sit in the window to keep Gage in place.

"I can bind her magic," Zia said.

"No thank you. She can't do anything right now. The council will decide her fate. Keep Gage inside. I will put Xiala into the bed of the truck. We won't make it back to Amber Mountain without a rest, but I can keep her back there, bound and warm for the rest of today's journey."

Suleima pulled Xiala smoothly into the bed of the truck. She shielded her with air, protecting her from the bumps, as well as the cold. Xiala glared at Suleima the whole time.

Zia fluttered to her side. "I can help. I can put her to sleep for a bit. It will not harm her. On my honor, no harm to her."

Suleima nodded. Moments later, Xiala was asleep.

Suleima climbed in the driver's seat of the truck. She was exhausted.

They drove for several hours before Suleima pulled off the road into another wooded area. "I'll go forage for something to eat. Gage, please stay here and protect Xiala. Zia, stay with him. I will be back in just a few minutes."

She ignored Gage's growl of protest and headed into the woods. Reaching out with her senses, she felt the nature surrounding her. She could feel Gage, Zia and Xiala out by the truck. Gage was currently pacing. She smiled, then continued. She sensed a small creek in the distance and small birds and squirrels moving through the trees. A rabbit, startled by her presence, though it was 40 or more feet away, scampered underneath a nearby bush. She continued to walk until she came across a wild berry bush. It was a bit too early for the berries to be ripe so using a small amount of her earth magic, she coaxed the berries to grow and ripen, so she could pick some for herself and her friends. She gathered as many as she could carry before turning back toward the truck.

She wasn't surprised to see Gage in human form again when she returned. She passed out the berries before seating herself on the open tailgate and started to eat.

"I'll drive while you rest," Gage said after finishing his berries. "Do you need to refill your power well?"

Suleima thought a moment before nodding. "I better. It'll probably knock me out for a few hours, though. How are you feeling? How are your ribs?"

"I promise I'll survive. They're sore, but mostly healed now," he replied.

She nodded and went to grab the supplies she would need to complete her ritual. She was conscious of Gage and Zia's eyes on her as she performed the ritual, but she blocked them out as much as possible to keep her focus on the magic as she performed it. Her magic stores were much lower than she had allowed them to be in a long time. It took a lot of magic to battle against Xiala, especially when trying *not* to hurt her, as well as trying to protect Gage and Zia.

By the time she finished, her eyes were drooping. Gage came to her side as soon as the last of the sparks fell, wrapping an arm around her to walk her to the truck. He helped her in before running around the truck to climb into the driver's seat himself. He pulled her to the center seat, and she laid her head on his shoulder, drifting off to sleep almost immediately. She never even heard the engine start.

Chapter 13

Suleima was groggy when she awoke. It took her a moment to realize where she was and whose shoulder she was lying on. It came back in a rush. She closed her eyes, taking in a deep, steadying breath, then sat up, looking around.

"Sleep okay?" Gage asked.

"Yeah. How far out are we?"

"About another hour or so."

She asked him to pull over for a moment, got out, and pulled on her earth magic, calling a few birds and sending them out. She needed the council to assemble immediately to determine Xiala's fate and so she could explain the recent developments. She jumped back in, sitting back for the remainder of the ride.

She was nervous about the reaction the council would have regarding her fae parentage. She could lose her position on the council. While she felt awkward about being chosen as their leader, she still valued her position and wanted to help the council make the magical community a safer place for all races and power levels.

She startled when Gage took her hand in his, absently rubbing the top of her hand with his thumb. "I hear you thinking loudly over there," he said with a smile. "The council will accept you. I don't believe any of them will think differently of you, knowing you have fae parentage."

She gave him a surprised look and he laughed.

"I'm beginning to anticipate your worries. But this one was easy. You would only send out that many birds if you were calling for the council. In order to explain why Zia is with us, and why Xiala's reaction is so poor. You are preparing to tell them what you discovered. Not that you would ever keep it secret anyway. And I know how much this council means to you. The council will accept you. They know your heart. We have fought beside you. While you may get a few raised eyebrows, I believe, in the end, they will embrace you, and you could very well be the beginning of a bridge between the fae and the rest of us."

When they pulled in front of the building where their council meetings were usually held, Suleima sensed the other council members inside. She turned to Gage. "I need you to stay here with Xiala and Zia again. Please." She wanted him with her and knew he wanted to be there as well, but she wasn't dumb enough to trust an unknown fae with Xiala alone, and she would not spring this on the council without some kind of explanation. She saw his intent to protest. "Dyna and Kaly are already here. I have allies. I'll be more at ease knowing you protect me from here." Suleima hesitated, her thoughts seeming to scream at her with all the doubts and fears she had not voiced.

As if reading her thoughts, Gage said, "You know you are still the same person now you were before we found out about your heritage, right?"

"But, how? I am half fae. Everything I know about the fae..." she started.

He reached out, taking her hand in his. "Does *not* change who you are as a person," Gage finished for her. "You are a strong, independent woman who cares deeply about those around her, even people you have never before met. It is rumored the fae are cruel. But that can't be true for all of them. And you don't have a cruel bone in your body."

Suleima forced a smile. His support meant the world to her. Movement in the bed of the truck caught her attention. "Xiala is beginning to stir. I must do this quickly."

Gage nodded.

Suleima gave his hand a gentle squeeze before turning on her heel, heading straight into the building and through to the council room.

The moment Suleima entered, all conversations halted. She nodded a greeting to everyone and motioned for them to take a seat. Kaly must have spoken with Gage through their connection because her face first showed surprise, then determination, and Kaly walked up and stood beside Suleima. Dynasira furrowed her brow at Kaly's defensive stance but stood and took her place on the other side of Suleima, clearly demonstrating support.

"Thank you," Suleima said to Dynasira and Kaly, "but please sit with the rest of the council."

They both seemed reluctant but walked to their seats and sat.

Lysom looked around before asking, "Where are Xiala and Gage?"

Suleima took a steadying breath. "Gage is waiting outside with Xiala. I asked for a moment to speak with the rest of you before they enter."

Chatter started up again, as everyone asked questions, but Dynasira cleared her throat and they quieted again.

"Information has come to my attention in the last few days. The entire council must be given this information and decisions made," Suleima said. She started at the beginning, recapping everything about the encounter at Sumar's through to the trip up the mountain and meeting with the Ice Goddess.

"I have no memories before I came to live with Erist. My earliest memory is waking up in my bed, at his home. I was eight years old at the time." She detailed the vision she was shown by the barbegazi. "I was able to understand the barbegazi when he spoke in his language. The Ice Goddess explained that while my memories were taken, my skills with their language were not affected. I cannot deny the truth of the vision."

Gasps echoed around the table.

"Did I hear you right? Part fae?" Dynasira asked.

"Until now, there has never been a manifestation of fae power in me. I've never been able to access it. According to my mother, I didn't have any fae magic within me, only the shamanistic magic of my father." She took another steadying breath. "The water spear I told you about at Sumar's home, I believe now was me. I also shattered a tea kettle and cup in my sleep. I am completely untrained in the use of fae magic, so unconsciously is the only way I've been able to access it so far."

Everyone began talking at once until Dynasira let out a piercing whistle. "Please shut up and let her complete the story."

Suleima smiled gratefully before pushing on. "On the way back down to the truck, Gage and I encountered another fae. A pixie. This pixie said the Ice Goddess sent her to help me learn to use my fae magic safely and properly."

"That pixie could be lying!" Lysom shouted, before being silenced by a piercing look from Dynasira.

"She very well could be. However, I don't believe she is. I am also not dumb enough to allow her access to this council or anyone else without knowing protections are in place." Suleima paused. Her senses alerted her that Xiala was waking and beginning to struggle at her bonds. She quickly moved on to Xiala's reaction to the fae and the fight which ensued. "The fae kept her word. Xiala was sleeping, but now she wakes. She is struggling against the bonds I placed. As a council, we need to decide the best course of action for her, and if you deem it so, for me."

"Wait!..." Dynasira protested.

Suleima held up her hand to stop her. "I will be returning to the truck to sit with Zia and Xiala. The council can make whatever decisions they see fit. Gage was present for the entire trip and he can answer any questions. I'll send him in now."

She walked out to the waiting truck.

"Why are you not staying inside with the council?" Gage asked incredulously.

"The council needs time and freedom to discuss this information without me being present to prevent them from speaking their minds freely. I trust the council to make the best decision for them and the rest of who we represent," Suleima said calmly. The light touch of her hand on his forearm helped to calm her as much as she hoped it would help him. "Please be nice. Answer their questions. Send for me if questions arise which you can't answer. I'll wait with Xiala to discover both of our fates." Suleima placed a chaste kiss on his cheek, then walked past him to stop at the tailgate, where Xiala struggled to get out of her bindings. Just before Gage entered the building, she added, "Please play nice and listen to everyone's concerns. They are valid, even if you do not agree."

Gage's piercing blue eyes met hers for a moment before he nodded once, turned, and entered the building.

Zia flew over and landed next to her but as far from Xiala as possible.

"I can put her back to sleep if you wish," Zia said.

"No. She will behave herself. Right, Xiala?" Suleima responded, "She needs to be awake when the council decides to speak with her."

Xiala's eyes narrowed.

"If you fail to behave, I will have to bind you further. I can't trust you will not try to hurt me or Zia. I've done everything I can to keep you from permanent harm."

Suleima spun when Kaly's gravelly voice spoke up behind her. "Suleima may not do permanent harm, but I have no qualms about it." Kaly winked at Suleima before propping her hip against the tailgate.

"You should be inside," Suleima said.

"I said my piece. They don't need me in there. I cast my vote and also spoke up to the council to say my vote will not change no matter what anyone says. I came to help you out with her," Kaly pointed into the bed of the truck, showing Xiala her teeth. "And, to meet this fae. Also, Gage will keep me apprised of anything that comes up."

Suleima introduced Zia to Kaly. She noticed Xiala did fight less with Kaly sitting so close. Every once in a while Kaly would tilt her head, listening to whatever Gage was relaying, but then she would go on with her animated conversation with Zia about the forest where Zia lived and asking all the questions she could think of about the fae.

Zia was just as curious about wolves and was apparently not as intimidated by Kaly as she was of Gage.

Suleima was grateful she could sit back and not have to keep the conversation moving. Her stomach was in knots about the meeting happening just beyond the walls in front of her.

She hoped she would still be on the council after this meeting ended.

It wasn't long before Kaly tilted her head, listening. She stood suddenly, facing the door as members of the council began filing out. The council members each nodded at Suleima then stepped to the side. Dynasira and Gage were the last two to exit the building. Rather than step to the side, they each took up a place beside Suleima, Kaly stood behind her.

Hamanad spoke first, "It is my belief that I know you as a person and I don't believe you knowing all of a sudden you are half-fae would change your actions in any way. Being fae does not equal being evil."

Suleima nodded her thanks and looked to the rest of the council. They each seemed to agree with Hamanad's stance on her newly discovered parentage.

Lysom spoke up next, "As for you, Xiala, you attempted to use your magic to harm another council member unprovoked. You did succeed in harming another council member. For which, the council has unanimously voted you be removed. We will not bind your magic at this time. However, any further actions taken against any member of this council or under the council's direct protection will be met with dire consequences."

Xiala's eyes grew wide as he spoke and she redoubled her efforts to escape the bindings.

Suleima motioned for Zia to move behind her, then easily dropped the vines binding Xiala and the spell locking away her voice.

She need not have prepared to take another blow of magic from Xiala, because as soon as she moved at Suleima, Kaly grabbed her by the throat, stopping her mid-cast. "This is the only pass you get," Kaly's gravelly voice added to the menace pouring off of her, "Cast again. I dare you."

Xiala's face had turned a pasty white the moment Kaly's hand clamped onto her neck. She lowered her hand and released the elements she had called back into the earth.

Lysom stepped forward, "Xiala, I will escort you to your home. This council has given you its warning. There will be no other chances. This is not a threat. This is an explanation of the consequences you will face if any further acts against the council occur."

Lysom escorted Xiala to his vehicle and the two pulled away from the building, headed out of town.

Agron turned to Suleima. "Please come back into the council room, and we invite you to bring your friend."

Zia perched on Suleima's shoulder as they entered the building, following most of the council into the room. Gage and Kaly remained behind them, with Dynasira just in front of Suleima.

Everyone took their usual seats around the table.

Hamanad was the first to speak again, "Please introduce us to your friend."

"This is Zia. She is a pixie from the Phrostien Mountains. She was sent by the Ice Goddess, Zenisa, to help me learn to use the fae magic which has suddenly awoken within me. Right now, my use of it is unpredictable, usually appearing when I am in a high-stress situation without really knowing how to focus it. I do *not* want to be a danger to those around me, so I need to learn to consciously use this magic. Before now, the only magic anyone thought I possessed was shamanistic."

Zia spoke next, "I am versed in the earth magic of the fae, but also have a great affinity for water. This combination is one of the reasons I was chosen by our Goddess to accompany Suleima and help her learn to use her fae magic. I was also chosen because I am a curious pixie who shows no prejudice, unlike some of the other fae."

"When will you begin training Suleima?" Dynasira asked her.

"We will begin tomorrow," Zia answered, "She first needs to get some sleep outside of her truck. Good focus and concentration are essential. She must learn to call her fae magic, rather than the shamanistic magic she has learned to access ever since she was a child. It will take time. And, if I know anything about Solisa, she is not going to wait to put whatever plan she has into motion."

A few questions were posed by other council members before Gage stood, "We have had a long journey and a long few days. Suleima needs to rest. Any other questions can be answered later." Gage guided Suleima up out of her chair to her truck, where he tucked her into the passenger seat, Zia following close behind.

Suleima was dozing off before Gage climbed into the driver's seat. The adrenaline letdown and stress of the last few days sapped her energy the moment a chance to relax presented itself. As he started the engine, Dynasira appeared at his door, "Will you stay and watch over her tonight, or do you need to attend to your pack?"

"I'll stay tonight. Rest up." Gage turned the key, the engine roaring to life, before heading up the mountain to Suleima's cabin.

Before long, Gage parked Suleima's truck, and gingerly lifted her from the passenger side. She didn't stir, only snuggled in closer to him. He carried her to where the barrier of the ward was, before waking her fully, "We are nearly home, Sul. You'll need to let us in."

Suleima looked to where they were. "You may pass at anytime," her voice soft with sleep.

"But Zia?" he asked.

"Oh, sorry," she replied, yawning widely. Gage placed her on her feet but kept a steadying arm around her. She wondered if it was helping. It helped her to physically stay on her feet after being so exhausted, but it scrambled her concentration. Trying to focus, Suleima strengthened her ward and added an allowance for Zia to be able to pass through without harm. Before she took a step toward the cabin, Gage lifted her again and carried her to the door.

"I will sleep out on the porch," Zia said, going to work, piling up some of the leaves which had gathered in the corners, "This will make a perfect nest for me."

Gage nodded, before carrying Suleima inside and placing her on her feet. "Prepare for bed. I'll wait outside until you are ready." He turned on his heel and headed back out with Zia.

Suleima felt so sluggish. She had been able to rally some energy to meet with the council, but her energy was gone and she only wanted to sleep. She moved quickly, despite her exhaustion, and let Gage back in, before climbing into bed. His wolf entered and climbed up, curling at her feet to watch over her as she rested.

Chapter 14

The next morning, Suleima awoke, Gage still asleep at the foot of her bed. Not wanting to disturb him, she lay, watching the slow rise and fall of the fur on his side as he breathed deeply in sleep. He had come to mean so much to her. Her life had been in turmoil since Erist's death. Since before that, really, when Dirrin first became a danger. It certainly had not stopped with the emergence of this new threat, but when she was with Gage, the danger faded into the background. He made her feel strong and calm. Her confidence, when she would normally be timid, came from his presence. Knowing that he was there and would have her back in any situation, gave her peace of mind. He was the best man she had ever met, and Erist had set the bar pretty high. Gage meant so much to her, and yet, sometimes she wanted to throttle him.

Gage's eyes blinked open, and he caught her watching him. He jumped down off the bed to be let out to shift. While he was gone, she got up and readied herself for the day ahead.

By the time Suleima was putting breakfast on the table, Gage was walking in the door.

"Zia is still sleeping," he commented as he sat down at the table next to her. "What is the matter?"

"Something has been bothering me since yesterday…" she began.

Gage put bacon onto his plate and waited. She didn't say anything more. "What has been bothering you?"

She took a deep breath. She didn't want to yell, but she felt very strongly about this, "When I place a ward or shield, *do not* try to break through it!" She mostly managed to keep her voice level, mostly.

"Don't put up a ward or shield to keep me from defending you, and I won't break through it," he countered.

"You could have been hurt! You *were* hurt! If I hadn't pulled down the shield, you would've been hurt *more*!"

"I won't apologize for protecting you. I won't promise to never do it again. I protect what is mine. I won't stand back and watch you in danger," he countered.

"I'm not helpless! I can protect myself. *I* won't let you be hurt on my account!" She pounded her fist on the table.

Gage paused a moment, then placed his hand over her closed fist on the table. "I do *not* believe you are helpless," he said calmly. "I have *never* thought of you as helpless. You are one of the strongest people I know."

"Then *why* would you put yourself in harm's way?" she asked exasperated.

"An Alpha protects his pack. His pack is certainly not helpless, but that is the Alpha's job."

"I am not a wolf. I am not pack."

"You aren't a wolf, but you are pack. My wolf and I both agree on that. And yes, I protect my pack, but none so much as my mate." He squeezed her hand, catching the surprised look on her face when his eyes met hers. "I didn't want to discuss this during an argument, but now is as good a time as any, I guess. You are my mate, Sul. My wolf and I both feel it. The connection with you is strong. There's no question in my mind."

She turned her hand, twining their fingers together before speaking, "You can't expect me to stand aside and not protect my mate either." She raised her eyes to meet his.

Gage stood, tugged her hand so she stood with him, and wrapped his arms around her, breathing in her scent. "We will just have to figure out how to navigate that then," he said into her hair.

Suleima leaned back to look at his face, then reached up to place her lips on his. A chaste kiss, but full of meaning. Gage released a low growl before deepening the kiss, pulling her tightly to him. The quiet knock on the door a moment later, had him growling again, for an entirely new reason.

Suleima giggled, before heading to the door.

"Dyna is here," she told him, opening up the door.

Dynasira entered the cabin with a goofy grin on her face and gave Gage a light punch on his shoulder as she walked past and stole the piece of bacon off his plate. Zia zipped in, landing on the table and snagging a piece of fresh fruit.

Suleima thought she heard Gage mumble something about damned dragon shifter hearing and smiled. She grabbed some breakfast for herself and sat back down at the small wooden table.

"So what is on the agenda today?" Dynasira asked in between bites of food.

"We need to work on your ability to use your fae magic intentionally," Zia said. "Although I like it here, I miss my mountain."

Suleima nodded. "I will do my best to learn quickly, so we can get you home."

"It will not be easy for you," Zia continued, "Your natural instincts will be to pull from your shamanistic power. It may be easier for you if I bind your power over water."

"Nope," Gage said emphatically, "We are not going to experiment with that."

Suleima chimed in, "I would like to try to learn without binding any of my elements. That is a crutch. In a real-world situation, I would not have those powers bound, because I won't agree to cut off any of my shamanistic powers permanently. I have to learn to differentiate the two power sources. That will be part of the learning process."

"I agree," Zia said, "but I wanted to present the option."

Chapter 15

They finished breakfast before the four of them headed out to the meadow that Suleima often walked to. The sun was shining brightly, without a cloud in the sky. The colors in the meadow were vivid, flowers and leaves and wildlife each competing to outshine the next.

Zia fluttered in front of Suleima, "When you reach for water with your shamanistic powers, what are you reaching for?" she asked.

"It is usually easiest for me to reach for a nearby water source and call from that source to me. I can use the water in the ground or air in a pinch, but it is much simpler to pull from the water in a lake or stream," Suleima answered.

"Can you pull water from yourself?" Zia continued.

"Pull water from within my body?" Suleima asked. At Zia's nod, she replied, "No. I have never tried to use the water within my own body. I have pulled water on the surface, like if I am damp from the rain, but usually, a more abundant source is in the ground or air to pull from nearby."

"Good," she replied, "Fae magic comes from within, so in theory, it should be like using a different muscle entirely when you use your fae magic." Zia paused a moment before continuing, "I felt you use the fae magic when you were fighting with Xiala. Those waves were impressive. Can you remember how you accessed it?"

"I remember feeling something different. When I reached out, it felt fluid and cool. But it disappeared. Then Xiala hit Gage with that fireball and tossed him with wind. I had to do something and it just happened. I was as stunned as you were."

"And with the water spear?" Dynasira prompted.

"I didn't even know I had done that. I originally thought it was Dyna who had done it."

Zia replied, "The fact you feel it so differently will help you in the long run." Zia got a glint in her eye, "You have only ever been able to access it when someone you care about has been in danger."

"No," Suleima's tone brooked no argument, "You will not endanger Dyna or Gage. I will either learn to use it consciously or not. I won't have them targeted to provoke me."

Zia put her arms up protectively. "Okay, got it. No direct danger to your friends." She winked at Suleima before continuing, "But did you feel that?"

Suleima tilted her head and her eyes widened. She had felt something. She closed her eyes to concentrate her focus inward. There was that cool, fluid feeling again. But when she reached for it, it disappeared. She explained it to Zia.

"Stop reaching for it," Zia said. "Fae magic is not like shamanistic magic. Fae magic just is. You let it flow. The magic is within you. You never need to refill your fae magic. It is not a resource of the elements around you. It is a resource within yourself."

Suleima closed her eyes again and searched for that cool and fluid feeling. It stayed out of reach.

Zia flitted over to her, landing on her shoulder. Zia knocked on Suleima's temple. "Stop reaching for it!"

Gage growled.

"Knock it off, Alpha. I'm not hurting her."

Gage growled again. Zia jumped off of Suleima's shoulder and flitted over to Gage.

Suleima shot a stream of water, knocking Zia away from Gage.

"Good job!" Zia praised.

"I said, do *not* use my friends to make me use my fae magic." Suleima's voice was hard.

Zia shrugged. "It worked, did it not?"

Suleima forced the pixie to fly higher by sending a spurt of water from below her.

Zia laughed, then threw water in Suleima's direction. Instinctively, Suleima pulled an air shield around her.

"Nope," Zia said. "Stop relying on your shamanistic magic. Use water to redirect the water I sent at you."

Again, Zia fired water at Suleima. This time it hit her square in the face.

"It's not always there!" Suleima said frustrated.

"It is. You just have to learn to access it." Zia sent water at Suleima multiple times, and each time it hit her in the face.

"I'm not getting anywhere right now. Let's break for lunch," Suleima said.

"Fine," was Zia's exasperated response. "I had high hopes for you. You threw that water at me so quickly, I thought maybe you had figured it out already."

Dynasira spoke before Gage could. "Look fairy, either be encouraging, or go. We will help her figure this out without you. Put-downs are no way to teach, and they will not be tolerated here."

"Then she needs to learn, to make me stop," Zia said snidely.

Gage snatched the fae out of the air, ignoring her squeak of surprise, "You better figure out a new teaching method."

Her wide eyes showed her fear plainly and she nodded quickly.

The walk back to her home was uneasy. Frustration overwhelmed Suleima, and her friends were angry. She knew she needed to get a handle on this power if she was going to ever be safe to be around. She didn't know if she would get angry and lose control of her fae magic, and she certainly didn't want to hurt anyone unintentionally.

They went into the cabin and Suleima went to the area that served as her kitchen, absently starting to make lunch. She was so focused on the task at hand, she didn't realize Zia and Dynasira had left.

Gage approached her from behind, wrapping his arms around her and burying his nose into her hair, inhaling deeply. Defeated, tears began to fall despite her efforts to hold them in. Gage's arms tightened around her, before turning her in his arms and pulling her into him again. She buried her face in his shoulder and sobbed. Gage bent, lifting her into his arms, and sat on a chair, holding her in his lap, letting her cry, comforting her as best he could by rubbing her back.

When she was finished, she mopped up her face with a nearby towel. "I'm sorry. It's just so frustrating!"

Gage brushed a stray lock of hair from her face and touched his forehead to hers. "You will figure it out. It's new. It will take time. You have an immense talent with magic. This is just different from what you know."

"Why did Erist keep this from me?"

Gage sighed, "He thought he was doing what was best. You didn't have access to any fae magic before now. Everyone who knew thought you only got magic from your father, so there was no reason to upset your world by telling you differently."

When she was about to speak again, he pressed his lips to hers to quiet her for a moment. "What is done is done. It can't be changed. Wishing it was different won't change it. We just need to move forward and push through. Maybe someday you will figure out why, but there's no point in questioning it now. We need to figure out the how."

She gave him a small smile. "You are a very wise Alpha."

Gage linked his fingers with hers, their gazes connecting, "Where is the fluid feeling now? Can you find it?"

She didn't close her eyes this time, unwilling to lose the connection with Gage. "I found it," she said quietly.

"I'm thirsty," he said, "Can you make some water come out of the sink pitcher pump?"

Her brows furrowed with her effort.

Gage dropped one of her hands and touched her forehead at the wrinkles. He dropped a small kiss on her lips and said, "Don't try so hard."

She took a steadying breath and purposefully relaxed the muscles in her face and body. She focused on his need for water and gasped as a trickle of water fell from the pump into the sink. She smiled broadly.

"Try again," he said softly.

She gave a small nod and tried again. The trickle was a little faster this time. She closed her eyes to increase her focus, smiling when she heard the water moving a bit faster. She cupped her free hand, imagining the water falling into a bowl as she would usually do, but the trickle stopped.

"Fae magic is not like shamanistic magic," Zia said softly. Suleima had not heard or sensed Dynasira and Zia returning, because she was so focused. "The water will not bend to your will. It only follows its natural flow." She paused a moment and flew closer, "You did well. I could feel you using your fae magic. You were able to access it. Build on that. But don't force the water to do what you wish."

Suleima smiled at her and nodded.

Zia landed on the table. She tapped her small finger on her chin, thinking, before speaking again. "With your shamanistic magic, you make the elements do things that they normally would not do. Fae magic can only guide the elements. We cannot make it do something it would not do in nature. You could have pulled the water from the pump into a nearby glass, but to make it collect itself with no container is not natural for water. You can spray water, even a jet of water, like the 'water spear' you described from the lake house. You can make it wave, like you did against Xiala. You could even change the buoyancy of the water and walk on it. It's hard for fae to use water around us. We conjure it from within. From what I have seen, your shamanistic and fae magic for water are cooperating. That's new territory. You being the first half-fae, half-shaman I have ever heard of... this could be very interesting."

As they talked, Dynasira waited by the door. When Suleima stood to finish preparing lunch, Dynasira stepped forward, tripping over the journal the two of them retrieved from Erist's home. Dynasira stopped, looking down at the book which hadn't been there a moment before, then shifting wide eyes back to Suleima.

Suleima slowly and gently set down the plates she held, then brushed her suddenly damp palms over her hips. She stepped forward carefully before bending down to pick up the worn leather journal. It warmed to her touch. She raised her gaze to Gage, then Dynasira. "I guess I should open this, right?"

Gage pulled out her chair, motioning for her to take a seat. Once in place, instead of sitting next to her, Gage stood behind, placing his hands on her shoulders.

Suleima laid the book flat on the table and placed her hand on top, taking a deep breath, then carefully opened the cover.

The thick pages were yellowed with age. She could feel the magic pulse within the handmade paper. The low vibration emanating from the pages made her fingers tingle and itch to draw on her magic. She turned page after page, only to find they were blank. Suleima furrowed her brow. Could nothing go easy for her right now? Yet another puzzle. Erist would never hide a blank journal. And she could feel the magic calling to her, but it seemed to be foreign. She didn't understand what it was asking her to do to unlock it.

Suleima tried to pull with earth, but the book visibly moved away from her on the table, repulsed by the infusion of magic. She pulled on air, the gust of wind turning the pages, showing each one still blank, before slamming itself closed. Despite her desire to throw the offended book against the wall, Suleima delicately lifted the book from the table and placed it back under her bed. Her friends' questioning expression when she turned around made her sigh. "I have enough frustrating things going on right now. Too many puzzles to figure out. The journal will have to wait."

Not waiting for a response, she walked the few steps into the kitchen and finished preparing lunch.

They ate a quiet lunch, before returning to the meadow for Suleima to practice some more. By the end of the afternoon, she had a few successes and many failures, but she was looking forward to trying again. Zia was a more effective teacher this time. Gage and Dynasira sat nearby watching. They were a constant source of support for her and Gage only growled a few times at Zia when she got frustrated and impatient with Suleima.

They ate a hearty dinner. It was already getting a bit late in the evening when Gage stood from the table. "I have to go to the pack house tonight. I need to finalize the rotation at the campsite this week and check in on the pack. Will you be okay here?"

She nodded shyly and stood as he took her hand. She walked him out to the porch, leaving Dynasira and Zia inside. He drew her into a hug before giving her a gentle kiss. "Do you want a ride to town?"

"Thank you, but no," he answered, giving her a final kiss. "I'll see you tomorrow."

She watched as Gage walked into the trees and sensed his shift. She waited on the porch until his shift was complete and he headed down the mountain.

When she couldn't sense him anymore, she walked back into the cabin. Zia and Dynasira were sitting at the table talking, but it abruptly stopped when she entered.

Dynasira stood and walked over to her, wrapping her in a rare hug, "I'm so happy for you," she whispered, "Hang on to that one. He's a good man."

Suleima blushed and backed away. "He is a good one," she said shyly.

Zia was full of questions. The curious pixie peppered Dynasira with questions about being a dragon before turning her gaze to Suleima. "What's with the dance with the sparkles?" she asked.

"Huh?" Suleima asked.

"When you spin and dance in the sparkles. I've seen you do it a couple of times. Here and when we were driving down from Phrostien." Zia bounced on the balls of her feet as she stood on the back of one of the wooden chairs in the kitchen. The pixie was always in motion. If her wings weren't fluttering, she was bouncing or jumping. And, *always* talking.

Suleima smiled. "That is called the Ritual of Alucenia. All shamans use the ritual to call to the elements and refill our power wells." She walked to her cabinet and pulled out the soil, incense, and charcoal. "I call to each element using each of these and a bit of water from the well. Smoke begins to billow out of the ritual bowls." Suleima pointed at the two unpainted ceramic bowls with pestles still on the shelf in the cabinet. "Next orbs form, each taking the colors we associate with the elements. Green for earth, blue for water, red for fire, and yellow for air. Those orbs float in the direction which is associated with each element as well. The smoke vanishes, but as the orbs slowly dissipate, the energy from each orb joins above me. It rains down, filling me with the elements I called."

"Why must you do that? And why are you so sleepy after?" Zia asked.

"Shamanistic magic isn't like fae magic. You can't run out of fae magic, right?" When Zia confirmed it, Suleima continued, "I can only carry a finite amount of magic within me. I need to be careful which spells I use because I could run out of power and be unable to cast. There is a cost to use the elements. A sacrifice or payment must be made. The cost I pay is having my energy sapped and I must rest to recover before I can cast again. I can put off sleeping if I limit the amount of magic I refill. If my reserves run too low and I fully charge, staying conscious after can be a huge challenge, and I will sleep for many hours. It is a balance. For the privilege of the power, a payment is required."

Chapter 16

It was the wee hours of the morning when Suleima felt something odd and stopped mid-giggle. She stood, holding her hand out to Dynasira and Zia to hush. Something was outside, just beyond the ward. Suleima reached out with her senses, detecting a wrongness, but nothing indicated what it was. She noticed that the usual forest creatures moved away from her home. A predator of some kind lurked out there. It moved too fast for her to parse out what it was. Something unnatural for sure. It buzzed in and out of her range of perception.

Suleima motioned for Dynasira and Zia to stay out of sight and she erected an air shield before opening her door and walking out onto the porch. Whatever was outside was fast. She sensed a blur but was unable to pinpoint a location or even tell what type of creature.

Then she smelled it. Smoke. A fire in the forest, at the edge of her ward. It was off to the side of the cabin, out of sight from the porch.

Energy was being sucked from her ward, taking it down quickly, while the flames from the fire picked up intensity. Suleima had designed this ward to feed periodically from her, while she was on the property. It required much less maintenance that way. downside, as the energy was sucked away from the wards, it pulled her energy as well. She felt her knees go weak, and abruptly cut off the magic supply to the ward, and it fell moments later as the last of its protection was drained. The fire ate up the ground, heading straight for her home.

Suleima did her best not to panic at the sudden vulnerability of having no ward to protect her. She used power well sparingly, as it was now dangerously low. She saw Zia flutter at the corner of her eye, and Suleima took a steadying breath. A weak stream of water flew from her to the fire. This water seemed to repel the fire. It backed away from her fae water magic. If her shamanistic water only seemed to enhance that fire, it had to be fae fire.

Despite Dynasira's protest, Suleima took another step out into the yard. "Kylin? Is that you?"

A wicked cackle was the only answer, but she knew the voice making that sound.

"Dyna, help Zia with that fire please," Suleima said calmly, and took another step into her yard, followed by another. If Kylin was using fae fire, if that is what she was given by the Sun Goddess, her fire would easily blast through the air shield Suleima currently erected around herself. Something needed to be done. She lacked confidence in what she was about to try, but there was nothing to lose. Suleima felt for the fluid cool feeling, instead of reaching for it, she molded her air around it, cradling it. In her mind's eye, she watched them swirl together, using her air, she pulled the water into her shield, using air as its container. The image of the forest through the shield rippled, like looking through water. Hoping it was enough protection, she took another step forward.

Kylin stopped right in front of her, about thirty feet away. She juggled a fireball between her hands. Kylin looked fifteen, the same as she had the last time Suleima had seen her. The only difference was her hair; it was now white-blonde, whereas before it had been a deep shade of brown. Same green eyes, same cherub smile, though a coldness reflected in her eyes, a sinister tilt to her smile that brought a chill to Suleima. It had nothing to do with the shield's distortion. The Kylin she knew was no more.

"Miss me?" Kylin asked.

"What happened to you?" Suleima responded, "Why?"

"I wasn't ready to die, and Sumar wasn't ready to lose me. He made a deal." Kylin shrugged as if it was no big deal.

"Sumar helped you become.... this."

She laughed without mirth. "No. He chickened out at the last minute, but Solisa saw something in me. She helped me to transcend," Kylin spread her arms out wide, the fireball floating above her right hand.

"You were at Sumar's house when I visited," Suleima said, hoping to keep Kylin distracted while Dynasira and Zia handled the fire.

"Yes. I don't know how you managed to escape. But then again, Sumar is not what he once was," she added a terrifying giggle at the end.

Suleima saw Zia was making some progress with the fire, but she couldn't see Dynasira. She took a moment to reach out her senses, finding Dynasira in the sky above Kylin. She only hoped that Dynasira would stay put. Her attention went back to Kylin as she began juggling that fireball again. Then the fireball vanished into thin air and Kylin's eyes turned a deep black.

The next moment, a fireball, much more potent than the one she had juggled, was launched in her direction. It was black and red swirled together. When it hit her shield, the fire sizzled and the water in the shield shimmered. But it held. Dynasira screeched.

"Go!" Suleima shouted at her as the shield took another hit and held, but barely.

Dynasira flew off, toward the pack house.

The last thing Suleima wanted was for Gage and the pack to end up in the middle of this. She needed to end it quickly. The fire was nearly out, and Zia had moved out of her line of sight. She pulled at the dirt below Kylin.

Kylin shifted out of the way. It was a move Suleima used since she first learned to defend herself with her earth magic. Suleima lifted the dirt and encapsulated the fireball, attempting to smother the flames.

Kylin fed more power into the fireball, fighting off her attempts to smother it. She launched the fireball at Suleima.

Suleima dove out of the way, using a burst of air to push the fireball into the air, so it did not hit her house. She took precious resources to push the fireball toward the meadow and dropped it into the center where it would do the least amount of damage.

Suleima redirected her attention in time to see Kylin rush at her. If Kylin touched her she would kill her. Suleima shifted her weight and ran straight toward Kylin.

Kylin's eyes widened in surprise. Suleima slid to the ground, under Kylin's reach. Suleima pulled with her earth magic to slide further than normal, then jumped back to her feet and spun around.

Kylin screamed with frustration, spinning back around to face Suleima, only to be hit from behind by a stream of water. When Kylin spun to find the source of the water, the forest beyond was the only thing visible.

Suleima saw Zia flit away out of the corner of her eye. Movement in a new direction alerted her to Zia's new location. A moment later, another spurt of water came before she vanished again.

The pixie moved very fast when she wanted to.

Kylin kept spinning, searching for her invisible assailant.

Taking advantage of the distraction, Suleima pulled from her shamanistic water magic. She sent a bubble of water at Kylin and surrounded her with it.

While Kylin fought hard to escape the bubble, Suleima ran beyond the tree line. Suleima kept sending more water to the bubble to strengthen it, but it was a losing battle.

Suleima heard Dynasira's screech when she returned, spitting her own boiling water at Kylin, just as Kylin broke through the water bubble. Zia continued to flit in and out of sight, throwing water at Kylin. The combination drove her away from Suleima's house. Suleima sensed the pack's approach.

Suleima felt the cool fluid feeling again, she did her best to crudely mold it with her shamanistic magic and sent a spear of water at Kylin. The spear pierced her shoulder and Kylin screamed again, then using her speed, vanished out of Suleima's sight. She vaguely sensed Kylin's movement, in the opposite direction of the pack.

Suleima sank to the forest floor, her magic reserves dangerously low. Dynasira and Zia emerged into the clearing in front of her cabin. Dynasira shifted as soon as her feet hit the ground. "I don't feel her now," Suleima said, her voice breathless after that fight, "She headed away from the pack. They should be safe."

"They'll be angry they missed the fight," Dynasira commented.

"Good," Suleima responded. "That's not a fight they should be in."

"My pack and I will be the judge of that," Gage spoke as he stepped up behind her, the wolves spread out behind him, ever watchful. He reached down, taking her hand and helping her to her feet. He placed his arm around her waist, propping her up. "Fan out and form a perimeter. Make sure there are no other surprises."

"I'll head out to the meadow. I saw smoke," Dynasira commented.

"I sent a large fireball to the meadow. Figured it was the safest place. The lake was too far for me. Hopefully, it has done minimal damage."

"I'll help Dynasira take care of it," Zia replied, following her deeper into the forest.

Suleima stumbled after a few steps, and Gage lifted her into his arms. She started to protest until his growl stopped her. She was tired; she would allow him to take care of her. She dropped her head onto his shoulder and sighed.

"You aren't helpless. Neither are we," Gage said. "My wolves and I are not fragile. We can help you."

"I couldn't stand if anything happened to you or anyone else in your pack," she whispered, "especially you."

His grip tightened on her momentarily, before he nudged the door open and carried her inside, placing her on her feet near her cabinet of supplies. "And how would I feel if something happened to you?" he asked softly.

Suleima closed her eyes, "I know."

"Then let me help you," he pleaded.

"This is going to exhaust me," she said, taking the ingredients from his hands, as he pulled them out of the supply cabinet for her.

"I'll keep you safe while you sleep," he replied, covering her hands with his briefly before stepping away, giving her room to complete her ritual. "We will take you to the pack house. The ward you placed there is still intact. Dynasira and Zia can come as well. Finish what you need to, and I'll get you there safely."

Suleima nodded and smiled, placing a gentle kiss on his lips. "I know you will."

She next awoke in a strange room. Suleima looked around, taking in the earth tones decorating it and the soft glow from a lamp across the room. She couldn't remember how she got here. Brow furrowed, she reached out with her senses. She found Gage nearby, as well as Kaly, Dynasira, and Zia. She also sensed a few other wolves outside. The pack house. She vaguely remembered Gage saying he would bring her here. She slowly sat up. Between the battle with Kylin and charging her magic resources after running so low, her body felt like it had been through the wringer.

Suleima's awareness informed her that Gage was coming up the stairs and down the hall before he entered the room. "Morning," he said.

"How long was I out?" she asked.

"Almost a day. A few more hours, and it will be breakfast time," Gage answered, sitting next to her on the bed. "The pack is patrolling past your house. There's been no further sign of Kylin. We haven't been able to pick up her scent or any hint to indicate which direction she came or went from. The dragons are searching from above, but they haven't found anything either."

"If anyone does come across Kylin, they need to stay far away from her. She was able to pull energy from my wards to take them down and drained me right along with it. If she touches a wolf or dragon, she could kill them easily, just by touch. Not including what she can do with her magic. I need you and the pack to stay away from this."

Gage took her hand in his, "Never going to happen. If you are in this, my wolves and I are in this. We managed to help take down monsters in the battle with Dirrin. We have learned a lot about other magic users and how to deal with them. This is no different."

"But..." Suleima began.

Gage placed a quick kiss on her lips, "No buts," he interrupted, "The dragons aren't going anywhere, either. You better get used to the fact that you aren't alone. You don't have to take these things on by yourself."

"The danger—"

"—is there for all of us. We aren't willing to lose you, so I guess we will work together. It worked last time. I think we can make it work this time." Gage took her hand in his. "Come eat, and after we will talk more."

The smells from the kitchen had her stomach growling before she reached the stairs. Kaly, Dynasira, and Zia greeted her as she walked into the kitchen with Gage. A plate loaded with pancakes and another with bacon sat on the marble counter of the island in his large industrial-style kitchen. She piled a plate and headed to the small breakfast nook where the others sat, Gage shadowing her. She slid into the bench seat, and he followed immediately after, resting his arm behind her, their legs touching.

Kaly watched with a sly smile on her face as Gage interacted with Suleima, noticing Gage slide food from his plate onto hers, as Suleima was not looking.

Dynasira and Kaly kept exchanging glances, while Zia buzzed around, chatting incessantly about getting to meet all these new types of creatures.

Once Suleima finished eating, Dynasira and Gage brought her up to speed on the scant information they found while she slept.

"We need to come at this differently," Suleima said, "At this point, we know who is involved but not their motivation. We don't necessarily need to know where they are holed up right now. What we do need to determine is why. Why steal Dirrin's books? Are they looking to do the same as Dirrin? Or is there some other reason that we're blind to right now? I think the why is going to be the most important part of this equation. Why was the obsidian left behind?"

"Was Kylin elitist, like Dirrin, before she was turned?" Gage asked.

"She was fifteen when I was told that she died. As far as I know, she was not. I do know Sumar wasn't elitist."

"OK," Dynasira said, "Let's say that Kylin is not, and never was, elitist. I can understand her not wanting to pass at such a young age. Being turned so young, she could have been molded by this fire queen of the fae, so we need to consider what the *queen's* purpose would be, if she is puppeteering Kylin."

Zia piped up, "What was in the missing books? Do we know? It may be this has nothing to do with the fae and everything to do with what is in those books."

"His books were gone before we found the camp. I have no idea what was taken. I sensed the remnants of powerful protection spells on the chest and cabinet in his tent which were disabled but not triggered. Only someone at least as powerful as Dirrin could have gotten them out without triggering severe damage to themselves, the tent, and the surrounding camp."

"I assume the books would have more in them besides spells to kill off hundreds of people at a time," Gage said.

"You would be right on that, I'm sure. But I have no way of knowing what books he had. I believe at least some of those books are from the shaman who Dirrin went to when he left Erist, the one he killed, consuming their power for his own."

"Would any of the prisoners we have in custody know anything?" Dynasira asked.

"Dirrin used people until they were of no use anymore. Would he have included anyone in his plans? I'm not sure."

"Only one way to find out," Dynasira said, standing and heading for the back door.

Chapter 17

The pressure was palpable as Suleima entered the prison building, feeling the magic-dampening spells surrounding the facility. Gage let out a low growl, and Suleima reached out to take his hand.

"It's for our safety as well. If we can't access our magic within these walls, neither can those in the cells," Suleima said to comfort him, although she felt the same anxiousness at losing access to her magic.

Zia tossed a stream of water from one hand to the next, "It does not affect my magic."

Dynasira looked over at her surprised, "It's supposed to dampen all magic."

"Even you shifters have your magic tied to the elements, even if it's not one specific element. There is magic in the earth you harness to shift. Fae magic comes from within," Zia answered.

Suleima stopped, halting everyone's movements, "As a shaman, I harness the elements, but I pull the magic within to be used."

"So…why can you not use your shamanistic magic, since it is inside you, once you fill your wells?" Zia shrugged. "But this would be a great place for you to practice using your fae magic."

Suleima took a deep breath for a moment and tried to find the elusive cool fluid feeling. She shook her head, "Another time perhaps. For now, let's go find Yanima.

Dynasira led them into a room down a dim hallway. With no windows to add natural light, the fluorescent lights struggled to chase away the darkness within. The building itself seemed tainted by the evil it held. It held at least fifteen cells, most of which were occupied. She nodded at the Rojada clan member at the table at the front of the room, before walking to the back of the room. At the end, a thick steel door stood. Dynasira lay her hand on the door and closed her eyes, taking a deep breath, then reached down for the handle and turned the knob. She entered the room first, stepping to the side to allow Gage and Suleima to enter, Zia perched on Suleima's shoulder.

"Have I not been tortured enough!" Yanima shouted once she saw who entered.

Dynasira slammed the door shut behind them. "Never enough, Yanima. Never enough."

The magic-dampening spell pressed onto Suleima much more in this room and looked quizzically at Dynasira. She shook her head, indicating now was not the time.

Yanima stood abruptly and Gage stepped in front of Suleima in response. Suleima trailed her hand down Gage's back, signaling she was fine, before stepping around him to face Yanima. "How are you finding your accommodations?" Suleima asked.

"Get out."

Suleima kept herself between Gage and Yanima. "Is that any way to greet old friends?" Suleima said.

"Old friends? You locked me up in here and bound my powers!" Yanima's shout echoed off the concrete and steel walls encasing her. The hatred she projected was so strong, it was another presence in the room.

"Well, that tends to happen when you try to kill your 'old friends.'" Dynasira interjected.

Suleima raised a hand to stop the argument before it began. "Yani," she said, "we need to talk to you. Ask you some questions. Are you willing to be civil?"

"Why should I speak with you? Why should I answer any of your questions? You killed Dirrin! You stole my magic! You ruined *everything*!"

"This was a bad idea," Dynasira said, "She will never cooperate."

"Yani, I know you are angry with us," Suleima kept her voice as calm as could, "We did what was necessary, and you know it. What Dirrin wanted to do would never have worked. Someone would have overpowered him one day. His plan was never sustainable."

"He would have been the most powerful shaman on earth! Nothing could have touched him!" She stomped her foot and pounded her fists against her legs.

Zia sprayed water into the air at Suleima's nod. Yanima's eyes widened.

"He never would have been a match for the fae. Had he approached them, they would have cut him down faster than I ever did. What books did Dirrin have hidden in his tent?"

Yanima pressed her lips together.

"What books did Dirrin have hidden in his tent?" Suleima repeated.

"What difference does it make now?"

"Because the fae may now have those books, and we need to know what was in them."

Yanima blanched. "No."

"The items in his cabinet and chest were missing when we got to his tent. We now know they are in the possession of an energy vampire at the least, the Sun Goddess of the fae at worst. I will repeat myself again. What books did Dirrin have in his tent?"

Yanima sat down hard on her bed and dropped her face to her hands. "We are doomed."

"What books did he have? What was in them?" Suleima asked calmly, sitting down next to Yanima while motioning with her hands for Gage and Dynasira to stay where they were.

"Dirrin wanted to make sure no one would ever be able to rise against him. He had plans."

"Plans to what?" Suleima prompted.

"The things in some of Erist's books... they should never see the light of day."

"Erist's books?"

"Dirrin planned to kill Erist that day. He wanted to get his hands on that book and Erist would never hand it over. If Erist hadn't enraged him, Dirrin would have taken his power as well. But the book.... It held spells of creation. There were spells in the book which can be used to alter creatures who exist now. Creatures with weaknesses that could be erased. He wanted to make himself invulnerable. It also had spells to make volcanoes erupt, and trigger earthquakes, tsunamis, tornadoes, and hurricanes. Not only that; he could trigger those things where no threat exists. He could create a fault line where none existed, a quiet mountain blown apart by a magically made volcano."

"So, he would have had the ability not only erase the weaknesses of his own, but the survival of anyone on the planet would revolve around his mood?" Suleima asked, incredulously.

"Anyone in his good graces would be safe," Yanima said. "But he did not have the key to access the spells in the book. Once he found it, he would hold the entire world hostage."

"And tell me again, why you thought joining him was a good idea?" Dynasira asked.

"If I was with him, I was safe."

"Brilliant," Dynasira said, her voice dripping with sarcasm, "And who did he plan to rule over, when everyone was dead?"

"People want to live. They would bend and fall to their knees to worship him as their God. And they would be richly rewarded for their loyalty and service."

"When you say a 'key'..." Suleima prompted.

"The book has some kind of magical lock on it. So, the fae can't access it."

"And if the fae find the key?"

Yanima visibly paled.

"Where was this key?"

"I don't know. Dirrin didn't, either. He found the book in a chest Erist owned. He carried that damn thing everywhere." She huffed and gave Suleima a nasty look, "If it hadn't been for you, he would have found the key by now."

Suleima's gaze darted to Gage. The empty chest which had been stolen from the tent the other night; it had to be the same chest. "What was so special about the chest?"

"How would I know? And even if I did, why would I tell you?" Yanima turned her back and refused to acknowledge them anymore.

They left Yanima's cell feeling defeated. While the information was helpful, now they needed to figure out what to do about it. Time was of the essence. They needed to find this key before Solisa or Kylin did.

"Could the answer to the key be in the chest? Is that why Kylin stole it?" Suleima speculated.

"Possibly," Dynasira responded. "There is no way to know without examining the chest, and we have no idea where it is."

Gage held up a hand. "I didn't personally know Erist. But from what I do know of him, he wouldn't have kept the book inside a chest that would point directly to the key. Especially if the spells in the book are as dangerous as Yanima said."

"You are right." Suleima looked between Gage and Dynasira. "He would have hidden it where only someone who didn't intend to use the spells could find it. It's in the journal."

"The key is in the journal?"

"It's the only thing that makes sense. When I needed information to stop Dirrin, when I needed to translate the spell, Erist always put me in the path of the answer. I still don't know how Erist knew about things that would happen long after his death, or how he came to influence things, but he has. Every time."

"So, we need to figure out how to unlock his journal," Gage said.

Suleima's shoulders slumped in defeat, but Gage slipped his arm around her.

"You can do this. Erist knew it would be you."

Once they were past the barriers surrounding the compound of cells, Suleima called birds to carry messages to the other council members to meet. Then Dynasira shifted and carried them back to Suleima's cabin.

When they landed, Suleima said, "I'll update the council. Dyna, can you take Zia home? Zia, we need you to speak with Zenisa. Ask if she knows anything about this key or where to find it, in case we are wrong. Also, see if the fae will help us against Solisa and Kylin."

Zia nodded.

A moment later, Dynasira and Zia were gone.

Suleima and Gage entered the cozy cabin. Gage held Suleima's hand in his as he walked over the table and sat, pulling her into his lap. He breathed in her scent, tightening his hold on her momentarily. He flexed his hands several times as they rested, one on her hip and the other on her thigh.

"I couldn't protect you in there," he said, almost to himself, "I couldn't feel my wolf."

"The spells surrounding the prisoners' compound are designed that way. We can't have the magic wielders and shifters able to use their powers and abilities," Suleima explained.

"I understand it. But my wolf and I couldn't protect you in that place." His hold on her tightened again, and she snuggled in closer, offering what comfort she could.

"No one was in danger, Gage. I'm fine. You're fine," she said, stroking her hand down his back.

He took several deep breaths, but his body remained very tense.

"What's going on in your head right now?"

"My wolf is very restless. Being confronted with that spell— he wants to mark you."

Suleima pulled away, looking at Gage quizzically. "What does that mean?"

"When a shifter, particularly a wolf, finds their mate, the wolf will bite them. Not only does the scar it leaves show everyone they are taken, but there is magic in it. It allows the mates to track each other, deepens their connection, even allows them to communicate when shifted," Gage explained, dropping his head to her shoulder, "Just give me a bit of time to calm down. I can get past this."

Suleima soothingly ran her hand down his back, thinking about what he just said. "I'm not a shifter. Does it matter?"

"No. Though I don't know how the tracking part would work for you," he answered after a moment. "I'm sorry. I may have to go for a walk if I can let you out of my sight... Right now, off of my lap seems to be too much for me to allow."

"What can I do to help you right now?"

"I don't know," he answered honestly.

"This may not help, but I am going to ask another question," she began, "What happens? Do you just bite the person?"

"There is a bit more to it than that," he replied, looking deep into her eyes, his hands repeatedly flexing on her. "But, essentially yes. It's how the mate bond is sealed."

"Like a marriage?"

"More," Gage took a steadying breath, "A marriage can end. A mate bond is forever. There's no going back once it is in place."

"I assume time is needed for the bite?" she said, "Like time to be together without an audience?"

Gage nodded. He was genuinely struggling.

Suleima took Gage's face in her hands, tilting his chin up so she looked directly into his eyes. She dropped her forehead to his and took a deep breath, "When the council meeting is over, will you return to the cabin with me?"

He nodded, "Of course."

"Once the wards are in place again, we will have as much time as we need."

Gage drew his head back, looking into her eyes, trying to read something in them.

She did her best to let her feelings for him shine through her eyes, her certainty, and her commitment.

His one hand released her leg and reached up to caress her face, drawing her down for a lingering kiss. Too soon, he released her with a growl. "The council will be arriving soon, and we need to figure out that damn journal." The low rumbling growl continued in his chest.

She gave him a chaste kiss and stood, bringing him with her, since he was still unwilling to release her from his hold. "We will be sending most of them out to gather any information they can about the key. It should be a quick meeting." She squeezed his hand when he nodded.

Gage didn't release her hand as she walked over to her bed. He helped her pull out the box holding the journal.

Instead of heading to the kitchen table, Suleima walked out onto the porch. When she set the journal on her lap, she could feel the warmth emanating from it, even through her jeans. Suleima opened the journal once more, but blank pages looked back at her. She curled her fingers, calling to the water she sensed in the ground beneath her. As before, the journal seemed to shy away from her magic, pulsing.

Suleima closed her eyes and guided her fae magic, producing a splash of water which bounced off of the page and right back into her face. "Ugh!" She wiped her dripping face with her sleeve and slammed the journal onto the porch beside her, her own growl rivaling Gage's.

When she would have stood to stomp off, Gage sat behind her, his arms encircling her waist and pulling her back against him. "What can I do to help you right now?" Her words from earlier.

"Make the words magically appear?" she responded.

"Magic is not my specialty." He nuzzled her ear with his nose. "What do you feel when you touch it? Is it the same pull you described when you found the journal?"

Suleima thought for a moment before responding. "No. It's completely different. The pull was a tug, like a string attached and wound up, pulling me closer and closer. This is.... Warmth is the only way I can think to describe it. The journal always feels warm."

"Warm as in cozy? Friendly? Or warm as in heat?" he asked.

"Heat."

"When you hit it with your shamanistic water first, did that seem to cool the heat?"

She shook her head. "No. It jolted me, a small buzz, not painful, but not pleasant either. An indication that whatever I was doing was wrong."

"Earth and air failed with your attempts before and now both shamanistic and fae water. There's only one element left." His voice was quiet, knowing what he was asking of her.

Suleima's hands shook as she reached for the journal again. She placed the journal back on her lap and closed her eyes. Erist had pushed her to use her fire. She frustrated him to no end with her fear of fire.

Suleima pictured the banked coals in her cookstove a few feet away, and she reached for the fire there. She pulled with her fire, the spark easily coming at her call. Suleima fought the desire to recoil from the heat she should be feeling in her left hand. She sensed the flame, the spark, as it sat in her open palm, but the scarring prevented the sensation of the heat from reaching her brain.

Wanting to end this as quickly as possible, she slammed the flame onto the cover of the journal and felt her ears pop as the magic cloaking the journal released.

They watched in wonder as the words written in Erist's script drifted over the page, and a small envelope appeared with her name in Erist's handwriting on the outside, his bold, sure strokes of the pen unmistakable. Her hands trembled again as she opened the aged envelope to pull out a piece of paper meticulously folded. She gently pulled at the folds of the slightly yellowed paper and took a steadying breath as she read.

Dearest Suleima, You cannot know what a treasure you have been to me in these last years of my life. You came to me at a time when I was lost and unsure what I would do next. Becoming a mentor was never my intention, but your arrival changed everything for me.

I have hidden this book where it will remain hidden and safe, no matter what the future holds. Dirrin has left us and I feel danger is ahead. In case I'm not around when you find this, know that you have made every sacrifice worth it. I could not love you more if you had been my child. I am privileged to be your mentor.

Protect the contents of this journal. You have grown to be the best of us, and you are about to discover how broad of a statement that is.

You will bridge the gap and hopefully make this world a better and safer place.

All the love, Erist.

Suleima blinked away tears.

She carefully refolded the letter and placed it into the envelope, setting it gently to the side, and ran her finger over the leather-bound tome in front of her. Gage's arms tightened around her as she opened the journal and read Erist's words. They carefully but quickly read through the journal.

Closing the book and tucking it into her arm, Suleima and Gage hiked out to her truck and headed to meet the rest of the council.

Chapter 18

Despite their delay with the journal, Gage and Suleima were still the first to arrive for the council meeting. Gage still kept near-constant physical contact with Suleima, holding her hand, a hand on her leg, or his arm wrapped around her shoulders. It wasn't long before Kaly and Lysom entered the building. Suleima heard Agron land just outside the building before shifting, then greet Hamanad as he arrived.

With everyone except Dynasira present, they entered the council room and took their seats. Gage didn't drop her hand until he pulled out the chair for her, then slid his chair closer before taking his own seat. Noticing the constant flexing of his hands on the arm of his chair, she shifted her left leg, so her foot crossed over his. Instantly, she noticed his posture relax and his hands fidgeted less.

"Erist's journal not only confirmed for us that the vision Vorelar showed to me was accurate, but it also discusses the key. There are few specifics, but one thing was very clear. The key is being protected by the jinn. They were entrusted to keep the key safe. I've gleaned from the journal that Erist was given the book from his mentor, who in turn received it from his mentor. It has been passed down this line of shamans, each of them protecting the book, and it has been this way for centuries. The spells contained inside are just as dangerous as Yanima indicated."

Hamanad spoke first. "Although I have no direct knowledge of this key, I can consult with our elders, who are incredibly long-lived. They may have some information which may help us. I must travel a great distance to see them, but I should get word back to you within a few days."

"Thank you, Hamanad," Suleima responded.

"I will consult the history books that were passed to me from my mentor," Lysom began, "Most of them have been passed down several generations. But if this is passed down only through his line of shamans, I don't know that I will have a lot of luck with my search."

The wolves and dragons, like most shifters, stayed to their own kind, and without any kind of casting magic, they didnt have books to pass down where spells or things had been written. But, Agron agreed to contact anyone he might know who may have such knowledge as well.

Suleima also briefed the council about sending Zia and Dynasira back to the Ice Goddess to see if she had knowledge of the key or if she would be willing to help in the coming fight with Kylin and Solisa.

As the meeting came to a close, Gage took Suleima's hand, keeping her from venturing too far, and walked over to Kaly.

"I'll be going with Suleima for a bit. Can you and Wade handle the pack for a bit longer?" Gage asked her.

Kaly tilted her head slightly, a question in her eyes, before she smiled brightly, "Absolutely!" She reached over and hugged Suleima tightly, ignoring Gage's growl.

They were quiet on the way. Gage was taking the drive slowly. Suleima was unsure if he was questioning what was about to happen, or if he was giving her time. Because of the permanence of the decision, Suleima took the time to seriously consider her choice. And the more she thought about it, the more certain she was.

Gage pulled her truck into her usual spot. They would still have a half a mile walk to the cabin. She was barely out of the car when he pulled her in for another lingering kiss. This kiss stole her breath. She held on to him as tightly as he held her.

When he pulled away, he took a very deep breath and blew out hard, trying to regain control. "Are you sure about this?" he asked.

"I have spent the entire ride thinking about it. Weighing each piece of the decision. The permanence, the seriousness, what it means. And, I have never been surer of anything in my life," she said with conviction. She looked away for a moment before continuing, "There's a lot that is unknown with me right now. Finding out that I am half fae—I don't yet know what that will mean for me. The question I have is, are *you* certain? With all the unknown..."

Gage kissed her again, stopping that train of thought. When he let her up for air, he said, "Fae or not, you are *mine*. There is no doubt in me or my wolf. You are my mate. If I could have claimed you while we were on Mt. Lucent without scaring you half to death, I would have. I have known that you were my mate since the day Wade showed up at the pack house to tell me that your cabin had vanished into thin air and you were nowhere to be found. I can't describe the feeling, the drop in my stomach, the panic I felt. I couldn't get here fast enough. And when you came walking out of that cabin, I wasn't sure if I could stop myself from running to you then. I held off. But barely."

Suleima smiled shyly. She placed another kiss on his mouth, and dropped her arms from around him, to lace their fingers together.

They walked a bit further before she spoke again. "Could my being half-fae affect the mating bond?"

"It doesn't matter to me either way." He squeezed her hand. "I've never heard of a shifter and fae sealing a mating bond. Like there are no half-shaman, half-fae before you, it is all unknown. We will deal with each challenge as it comes. Together."

She nodded her head and lapsed into silence for the rest of the walk, her mind still reeling with all the questions, but unwilling to them to dampen the happiness bubbling up inside.

When they reached the perimeter, where her wards usually stood, Suleima reached out with her senses. Finding nothing out of the ordinary, she dropped Gage's hand and turned to him. "I'll meet you inside, as soon as I replace the wards."

"I'll wait with you." Gage continued when he saw her about to argue, "I've felt the sting when you have placed wards before. I won't leave you out here alone." Gage cleared his throat. "I *cannot* leave you out here. Don't ask me to."

She nodded and knelt, burying her fingers into the lush forest floor, and closed her eyes. Gage was silent, but she felt his fingers curl against the wave of pain she knew he felt as she pumped her magic into the space around her cabin.

Once complete, Suleima walked into the clearing, just in front of her porch, Gage right next to her. She stirred the air, pulling soil and leaves from the ground, showering them over her home and yard. "As it was so long ago, it shall appear again. Time stands still and comes to an end. Until I wake, it shall not be. Cloaked from all, it can't be seen." She reached out and touched Gage's hand and placed her fingers gently over his eyes. She pushed a small amount of power to his eyes, then replaced her fingers with her lips.

When she stepped back, Gage opened his eyes and looked around. "That is amazing," he said, "It vanished, and now I can see it. Is that the spell you placed when Wade couldn't find your home?"

"Yes. After the banshee attacked I couldn't leave my home visible. I needed to recharge and I would be vulnerable."

"When Wade returned and said you were gone," he began, "I couldn't breathe. At first, I thought you fled and I may never find you again." He grasped her hands tightly, drawing her to him, wrapping her in his arms, breathing in her scent, "My wolf howled with pain. I knew then. You *are* my mate."

"I would never have left, knowing what was coming, knowing it was coming because of me. I would never have left you in danger," she said.

"I know that now, but the only thing I knew, at the time, was that you were gone, and I needed to find you. To protect you." Gage's hold on her tightened for a moment before dropping his hands to hers again. "Let's go inside."

Hand in hand, they walked up to the door of the cabin and entered. Gage closed the door, pinning Suleima against it and claiming her lips in a passionate kiss. His hands were on her hips, pulling her tightly against him.

When he pulled back, they were both breathless. He caressed her face with his right hand, looking deeply into her eyes. He paused a moment, his hand resting at her jaw, "Will you drop your glamor?" he asked gently, his voice barely above a whisper.

Had his hand not been touching her face, he doubted he would have noticed the subtle nod she gave before closing her eyes. He brought his lips back to hers as the glamor faded and the scars appeared. This kiss was gentler but no less passionate and heartfelt. He put all of his feelings into this kiss, just as she did. Nothing else mattered but the two of them together.

Suleima felt the sharpness of his teeth as they elongated, her nerves and anticipation sharpening along with them. His lips left hers, gliding slowly down to where her shoulder met her neck.

Time stood still. Pressure and pleasure warred as his teeth pierced her skin. There was no pain. Her knees buckled, but Gage's hold on her held her tightly to him. He licked the bite mark, sealing it, before lifting her in his arms and setting her down on the side of the bed, finding her lips again with his.

Chapter 19

Suleima stretched and smiled finding Gage asleep next to her when she woke. It was nowhere near the first time she woke up next to him, but this time, it was different. She moved to stand up and start breakfast, but Gage's arm snaked quickly around her, pulling her back against him and pressing a kiss to the bite mark on her neck. It was nearly healed already.

"You are beautiful," he said, tightening his arms around her, nuzzling her neck.

Suleima giggled and turned in his arms so she was facing him.

The glamor slid over her scars once more, and he placed his hand on the side of her face, "You don't need that glamor. Certainly not in front of me."

She dropped her eyes shyly. "I'm not ready for that yet. I may never be."

Gage tilted her chin, forcing her to meet his gaze. "You are beautiful and the scars helped make you who you are. They show your strengths. You have overcome so much."

She nodded, before tucking her head against his chest, relishing in his masculine scent. Since he marked her, her sense of smell seemed heightened. She absently wondered what else she may feel or get from this mark, and what he may experience as well. "Gage, I carry your mark on my neck to tell others I am your mate. What do you have to show that you are mine?" she asked.

He tilted his head, "I haven't thought about that." He paused a moment, "When shifters mate with another shifter, their bite mark is usually what each one wears. Of the shifters who have taken a human mate, only the human wears the mark. I'm not sure I have come across shifters whose mates are supernatural but not another shifter. If I have, I didn't know it. No one in the pack is mated to anyone other than another shifter or a human."

Suleima went about making breakfast and helping Gage to tidy up. They were stalling, neither ready to lift the cloak over their sanctuary.

Once the cleaning was complete, they shared another kiss before heading out to the porch. Suleima sensed Dynasira and Zia approaching. She closed her eyes and pulled down the cloak, revealing the cabin to any who ventured near.

Dynasira landed a moment later and smiled. "About time, you crazy kids!" she said, coming up and hugging Suleima, chucking Gage on the shoulder with her fist.

Suleima laughed at Dynasira's antics. It was nice to be lighthearted for a bit, but conversations needed to be had. Suleima sat on the porch bench; Gage taking his spot next to her while Dynasira leaned against the railing, with Zia standing on the rail next to her.

"How did things go with the Ice Goddess?"

"She knows nothing about a key to open the book we described," Zia began, "But she will approach the fae in her court to make your plea for help. Fae typically fight amongst themselves. But, if the book contains what we believe it does, the fae do not want it to become common knowledge any more than you do."

Suleima nodded. It was nothing more or less than she expected. Suleima filled Zia and Dynasira in on what she discovered in the journal and what happened at the council meeting. "It should be a few days before we hear anything from anyone."

Gage stood suddenly. "Something is in the woods."

Suleima scanned and felt the same thing as she did the last time Kylin visited. A blur of wrongness that moved too fast for her to pinpoint. Dynasira stood quickly and shifted, leaping into the sky for a better visual. Zia did the same, but hovered above the roof, staying out of sight.

Gage stripped off his shirt and began his shift on the porch. Suleima stared. He was shifting so much faster, and she could feel him, but he wasn't pulling on his pack bonds to shift more quickly, it was coming from her. When their gazes met, his eyes were violet, like hers when she was using magic.

She pushed away those thoughts, focusing on the matter at hand. Suleima grabbed her bow and arrows from inside the door, stepped off the porch, and took off in a sprint toward the lake. If she was close enough to the lake, the water would help to counteract Kylin's fire. This would also bring Kylin away from her wards and her home.

Gage stayed on her heels the entire way. She volleyed a few of Kylin's fireballs into the air above the forest so Dynasira could snuff them out and pulled a shield up to protect Gage from any she missed.

Kylin buzzed close for a moment and then retreated, over and over. She seemed to be trying to trick Suleima into following her deeper into the forest, but she wasn't about to do that. If Kylin wanted a fight, it would happen on Suleima's terms.

She pulled with earth to make her run as fast as possible. She skidded to a halt at the edge of the lake and pulled up another shield. She used her shamanistic magic to mold the water she pulled from the lake, but also tried to add in her fae water magic. The fae fireball would burn right through her shamanistic shield, but the addition of the fae water would hopefully slow it down.

Gage's anticipation buzzed through her head as he scanned the tree line, waiting for Kylin to appear again. She fumbled for a moment, the shield dropping in front of her as she caught a view in her head from Gage's perspective. She hadn't expected that. Redoubling her concentration, Suleima pulled the shield back up in front of her. She felt the fae water flow from her hand to swirl and twist, interweaving with her shamanistic magic in front of her. The shield rippled and shimmered in the bright light from the sun above the clearing. She tried to track the blur as Kylin paced, just out of view.

"Don't attempt to take her on physically, Gage," Suleima said quietly, knowing he was waiting for Kylin's appearance, "She's a vampire who feeds on energy, if she touches you, she can drain you. Prolonged contact would be fatal."

Gage huffed in disappointment.

She saw him in her mind, slinking into the forest, trying to pin Kylin down. Suleima grabbed him by the scruff, keeping him in place. "We don't split up unless there is no other choice." That she was able to visualize his planning now could help them coordinate their attacks, in most circumstances, but this was not one of those. However, the perspective changes were going to take some getting used to. The distraction caused her shield to falter again, but she regained control quicker this time, allowing her to stabilize the shield before it completely fell.

Gage growled, turning his back to Kylin. Suleima sensed the presence behind her. In her mind's eye, what Gage was seeing was clear. Her eyes widened and she shifted her stance, turning to see what came up behind them.

The large green figure stood on two legs and was easily fifteen feet tall. It looked as if it were wearing armor made from leaves and trees. Vines hung from its arms and swung around like tentacles. It stood on the far side of the small lake, knee deep, which would have to be nearly chest-high on Suleima.

Gage showed himself harassing the giant, green, humanoid figure, distracting him, and prepared to leap. If Gage focused on the plant creature, it left Suleima open to concentrate on Kylin. Except Kylin had disappeared.

Suleima pulled with her earth magic attempting to solidify the the mud at the bottom of the lake where the figure stood. He swung out with a tentacle in her direction and stomped his foot, easily pulling it free. She deflected the tentacle with air, but with her distraction, Gage had taken off toward the other side of the lake. Suleima fired an arrow at the giant mass of greenery, but a tentacle swung out, slapping it away easily.

Zia swept in, only to be hit with a tentacle, spinning in the air until she hit the trunk of a tree across the clearing. Suleima couldn't tell how badly she was hurt, but it was clear Zia would not be rejoining this fight.

Dynasira screeched as she dove down, spraying boiling water at the tentacled man, who screamed and pulled his tentacles back into his body. Gage snarled at the figure, who turned to face the wolf, only to be sprayed in the back again by Dynasira. Gage danced out of the way as the tentacled man trudged to the water's edge in his direction, both to distance himself from Dynasira and move closer to Gage.

Suleima threw up an air shield at the edge of the lake, stopping the creature and giving Dynasira another shot at him before diving out of the way of a fireball from Kylin, who was finally visible at the tree line. Suleima pushed a bit of air at the fireball, changing its trajectory. It sailed over the water and hit the creature in the same spot already hit several times by Dynasira. An inhuman wail pierced the air as Gage bounded around the shield and grabbed the creature by its tentacle.

The tentacle swung with Gage attached to the end, whipping over the water. Suleima felt for the fae magic she knew was there. She pictured what she wanted to happen in her mind's eye. As Gage's grip on the tentacle with his jaw failed, Gage went flying onto the lake's surface. Suleima watched as the surface of the water bounced with Gage's impact, softening the blow and catapulting him back the way he came, like a giant water balloon.

Gage grabbed the same tentacle as he soared through the air, his teeth sawing through, breaking it off and taking it with him. Suleima slowed his fall back onto solid ground with a cushion of air and turned back to Kylin who was readying another, larger fireball.

Suleima distracted Kylin, shooting another arrow in her direction as Dynasira switched targets, focusing her attacks on Kylin now. Suleima turned back to the green, armored creature. It was furious now that it had been injured. Its other tentacle swung wildly, striking out at them. It was all Gage could do to stay out of its grasp. Suleima pulled with her Earth magic, concentrating it on the tentacles, trying to bend them to her will. She tuned out the distracting flashes of vision she was getting from Gage, her focus pointed like a laser at the thick, green fines whipping around.

She changed tactics, realizing the creature was too strong. Suleima pushed her magic at the armored helmet on the creature. Pulling and twisting at it didn't work. It was part of the creature's body. Instead, she concentrated her magic on growth. She was finally seeing some progress as the helmet began to blossom. Suleima pushed harder and pulled in specific directions until the armor grew and covered the creature's eyes.

It began clawing at its eyes, unable to aim its tentacle strikes and distracted. Suleima targeted and pulled at the tentacles. She concentrated on the injured tentacle first, pulling it in toward the creature and wrapping it around the other arm, restricting its movement a bit. She pulled at the next one, using the longer tentacle that was uninjured to wrap around the legs of the creature. With the tentacles mostly out of the picture, Gage left her to go check on Zia.

Dynasira and Kylin behind her exchanging fireballs and boiling water were a distraction she could not afford, so she blocked them out.

Suleima shifted her focus to the armor covering the creature, pushing her earth magic, growing it. The tentacles were now wedged into the armor and more difficult to unwind. The creature bellowed in frustration. Suleima pulled harder, encasing the creature in its own armor prison. She threw a bit more earth magic at the creature, using it to root the creature in place, trapping it until she was ready to release it.

Dynasira positioned herself so Kylin was facing away from Suleima. Suleima tapped into the water magic she held. With Kylin distracted and unaware, she took her time, blending her fae magic and her shamanistic water magic with her air. She created a cyclone over the lake, the two elements working in conjunction. It took more power than she realized to move it, but she planted her feet and pushed. Slowly, the cyclone left the lake and moved past her over the land. Dynasira's screeching and Gage's howling masked the sound of the cyclone as it headed in Kylin's direction.

At this point, the sleeves of Kylin's jacket had burned away and there were flames halfway up her arms.

Suleima's magical stores were fading. The cyclone was so large, just keeping it intact was using up a lot of magic, moving it... well, she just hoped she had enough left.

She felt Gage lean against her to prop her up, giving her the strength for one last push. Suleima shoved hard with air, sending the cyclone straight for Kylin; its sheer size continuing its momentum as it picked up speed.

Kylin turned just as it overtook her. Her scream pierced the air, even above the sound of the cyclone. Suleima felt when Kylin escaped the cyclone, her energy signature was badly damaged as she zipped away. Suleima used her remaining power to unravel the cyclone. Gage's weight against her side was the only thing keeping her upright.

Dynasira landed and shifted, heading their way. "Zia?" she asked.

Suleima didn't have to reach out to find her; she saw what Gage had seen. "She's gone," Suleima answered, dropping her head.

"I'll gather her body and bring her to the fae," Dynasira said, heading to the trees where Zia had landed. "Gage, get her home and rested."

"I'll get there, Dyna," Suleima replied weakly. "Just give me a minute."

Dynasira walked over to the tree where Zia had landed and gently lifted the pixie. Her shimmery wings seemed to have lost their luster as they hung limply over the side of Dynasira's hand. She quickly shifted and headed to the east.

Suleima took a few steadying breaths. Gage kept to her side, giving her something to lean on as they walked home. She warned Gage that he would need to keep his senses peeled. She didn't have enough power left to reach out her senses. Even using Erist's trick to extend the use of her magic, creating and directing that cyclone used far more magic than she anticipated. It ended up so much bigger than she had originally thought it would be. As she thought of it, it must have been the addition of her fae water magic. She needed to use so much more of her air magic to contain it all.

It took much longer than she liked, but they finally made it back to the cabin. Gage shifted and dressed while she gathered the supplies to recharge. Gage sat on the bed, in his jeans, but left his shirt off, his head hanging low.

Despite the shaking in her hands, Suleima walked over to Gage and sat back on her heels at his feet, placing her hands on his thighs. "Talk to me."

"You need to recharge and rest," he protested.

"And I will. Talk to me," her tone brooking no argument.

"The yo-yo of emotions recently is just a lot." He took her hand in his, "Meeting you, discovering our connection, and completing our mating has made me incredibly happy. Indescribably so. Finding that my change is so much faster and less painful since the mating, has been amazing. The terror of you in danger..." he paused.

"I have been in danger since before the two of us met. And, I could say the same for you," she countered.

"Losing Zia. If only I would have..."

"Stop," she commanded sharply. "There is no 'if only.' There's only what is and the aftermath that we have to deal with. 'If only's will destroy you and me both. It's a lesson I work hard every day to learn. We have to lay blame where it belongs, on the perpetrators who are causing this. We haven't initiated attacks, we have only defended ourselves. We lay the blame at their feet, not ours."

Gage leaned down and pressed a chaste kiss to her lips, "Easier said than done. But I'll do my best."

"That's all I ask."

"Now, perform your ritual and recharge. I'll keep you safe while you sleep." Gage stood, helping Suleima to her feet.

Chapter 20

Hours later, Suleima sat straight up in bed, startling Gage who sat on the bed next to her, reading. She jumped to her feet and headed for the door.

"Not a mind-reader, at least not yet. What's wrong?" he asked urgently.

"Visitor," she said shortly, "A fae. I think the Ice Goddess. Dynasira is coming in hot behind her." Suleima's knees nearly buckled as her ward and cloak were ripped away from her cabin. Gage snarled and shifted.

Suleima tore open the door to confront the Ice Goddess, whose ice blue eyes swirled with turmoil and anger.

Dynasira landed hard on the ground behind the Ice Goddess and snarled her irritation. Gage's growl next to Suleima rivaled even the dragon's.

Suleima held up a hand, stopping Dynasira, and her other hand in Gage's fur at his scruff held him in place. She lowered her chin but refused to lower her eyes. This could be stupid and seen as a challenge, but Suleima would not cower before the Ice Goddess.

"My pixie was sent to teach you, *not* to *die for you*!" Zenisa screamed, her eyes blazing and her long, white hair blowing in a wind that existed only for her.

"Then I suggest you take up the issue with Solisa or Kylin and their plant creature, or whatever the hell it is!" Suleima stood her ground. She wouldn't cower from this woman.

Gage snarled when the Ice Goddess raised her hand, conjuring a ball of ice. Dynasira roared. But Suleima stepped forward. "Zia was helpful to us. She became a friend. We showed her respect and sent her home where she would have wanted to have her final resting place. She died helping defend us. She wasn't ordered to help us. If you want to blame anyone, you blame those who attacked!"

The ice ball flew in their direction. A burst of air from Suleima directed it to the side, enough that the only damage was to the far corner of her roof, where it skimmed by, taking several shingles with it.

"You are furious. So are we," Suleima continued as Zenisa formed a second ice ball. "I will not take kindly to another misdirected attack, Zenisa. You endanger my mate and my friend. You may be more powerful than I am, but I will make you regret your choice before I fall." Suleima pulled her elements, including fire. She gathered her fae magic as well. She held them all, unsure if Zenisa would attack, unsure if she would build a shield with it or fire it back at the Ice Goddess, but she would be ready either way.

Zenisa lowered her arm but didn't dissipate the ice ball. It hovered above her hand. "Mate? A half-fae, half-shaman with a wolf shifter for a mate and a dragon shifter for a friend?"

"Segregating yourselves from others only puts limits on you and your abilities. Working together, my friends and I are more powerful than I could ever hope to be on my own. Our weaknesses are strengthened by the strengths of others," Suleima said, taking a step off of the porch.

"Gage's wolves work together as a pack. Each individual wolf has its own strengths and weaknesses. The pack can bolster and support where an individual is weak, making the pack as a whole stronger. An individual wolf would have trouble taking down a bear. As a pack, they could take on several bears at once." Suleima took another step, "We are our own pack. Gage's wolves, Dyna and her dragon clan, as well as other clans, the jinn and shamans. Zia became a member of our pack, whether she intended to or not. Dyna, Gage, and I are prepared to fight for her, as they would fight for me. We work together to make this world a better place for everyone. Fae may be able to hide away. They may fight amongst themselves. But in the end, you are weaker for it. Take me out for the loss of Zia. But, my pack will come for you, as I would for any other member of my pack. You will be the one to suffer in the end. You may want to rethink your choice."

Zenisa dropped the ice ball. "For a young shaman, you are very bold. Arrogant."

Dynasira shifted. "Arrogant is as far from Suliema as you can get. She would—and has—put herself in front of danger for those she has never met." Walking past the Ice Goddess, heading for Suleima, she added, "Each and every one of us would die for her, and would not stop coming for you until you were dead, if you succeeded in harming her. I advise you not to try again."

Gage snarled his agreement.

Suleima held up her hand, "Enough." She turned to the Ice Goddess, "Zenisa, the creature is still in the woods, unless Kylin returned for it, which I doubt. I'll replace my wards, then I can take you to it."

Zenisa nodded and took a step back, behind where the ward had been.

Suleima walked out into the yard, showing none of her trepidation in approaching the Ice Goddess so soon after being attacked by her. Dynasira followed her closely and she felt Gage shift inside the house, before coming back out to observe from the porch.

As soon as the ward was back in place, Suleima stepped outside of it with Gage, and Dynasira on her heels. "I can take you to the creature now. I was able to trap it, but I had nothing left to do anything about it when the battle with Kylin ended. I can still feel it out in the lake."

"You trapped a fae?" Zenisa asked.

"It is some sort of creature made from vines and leaves. Its armor is organic. I used my earth magic to control the growth around its armor and, beginning with a tentacle Gage injured, I was able to wrest some control of the vine/tentacle and use it to begin to immobilize it. Once I could do that, I was able to root it into place," Suleima explained.

"You trapped a fae, using only your shamanistic magic?" she repeated.

"Yes. It was not easy, if you are thinking it was. Zia and Gage distracted it for a bit. Once it hit Zia and I saw her go down, I put everything I had into trapping it. One loss is too many," Suleima replied.

Zenisa shook her head, "You should not have been able to do that. We will need to talk further, shaman." Zenisa stopped talking as they entered the clearing where the lake was and saw the creature, still planted several feet into the lake. She turned her head sharply to look at Suleima. "You trapped The Green Knight?" She said its name like it was a title.

"If that is the creature in the lake, then yes," Suleima said flatly.

Zenisa eyed Suleima curiously and a bit warily. Zenisa solidified the water around The Green Knight's legs, then lazily walked around it, surveying its condition. She walked back to where the others stood. "Explain to me again how you managed this."

Suleima sighed and went over the events of the battle again. Zenisa stayed quiet, listening to the retelling. Her only reactions were the occasional raising of her blueish-white eyebrows and periodic shifting of her gaze to The Green Knight.

After the story, Zenisa walked back over to The Green Knight. She looked to Suleima, "Can you remove only the growth around his mouth, so he can speak?"

"I think so," Suleima said, slowly pulling back the growth which covered The Green Knight's mouth.

The Ice Goddess stepped up close to The Green Knight and nearly purred, "Oh Alder, how embarrassing for you. Bested by a lowly shaman."

"She is no ordinary shaman!" he protested.

"Oh, I see that now," Zenisa said, walking around him on the still-solidified lake. When she got to his back, where he had been hit by Dynasira's boiling water several times, she poked a long, spindly finger with a long, sharp nail through the foliage and into a wound, causing the knight to hiss in pain.

"He is trapped. There is no reason to provoke pain," Suleima protested, immediately building up the foliage around his wound, pushing the Ice Goddess's finger out.

"He is the enemy," Zenisa responded sharply.

"You attacked me at my home. Would you prefer to be treated in the same manner?" Suleima countered. "Respect and dignity will be shown to everyone. Or you may take your leave."

Zenisa altered her stance and Gage and Dynasira stiffened. A low rumble from Gage. "Easy wolf," Zenisa said, and his growl only got louder. Zenisa visibly relaxed. "I do not take orders any better than you would, Alpha."

"In my territory, around my mate?" Gage said. "You will."

The Green Knight laughed.

Suleima raised her hands, "Now is not the time. Continue to ask your questions, Zenisa. Or the council will decide on his fate, and you can return home."

"He is a fae. He is not under your council's command," Zenisa argued.

"Good to know," Suleima said dismissively. "When he is in our territory, attacking us, the council decides his fate. We may decide to hand him over to the fae to deal with, but again, it is *our* call. All your protesting is doing is delaying. Again, ask him your questions, or leave."

Zenisa visibly bristled at the command, but nodded before turning back to The Green Knight, "Why were you here? And what is Solisa planning?"

"When Kylin failed to destroy this simple shaman on her first visit, I was sent to help," he answered stiffly. "I had no knowledge of fae helping this shaman if that is what she is."

"You killed my pixie," Zenisa said, her hair blowing in the imaginary wind again as her power rose.

Suleima stepped between Zenisa and Alder, "I said question him, Zenisa. I will not repeat myself again."

The Ice Goddess took a calming breath and her hair settled back around her shoulders. "Why did you kill my pixie?"

The Green Knight's mouth tilted up in a grin, "She presented herself as a target. It was no more than squashing a bug."

This time Suleima bristled, pulling at her earth magic, tightening the armor further around him. "She was no bug. She was my friend. You will show respect, or you will no longer receive it."

The Green Knight coughed, unable to pull in enough air. Gage placed a calming hand on Suleima's shoulder, and she eased back on her magic, loosening the binds of his armor.

Zenisa laughed, "Not so easy, is it, Suleima?"

"It is not. That is why we must. If we do not show respect, then we are no better than them," Suleima responded, "And nothing I have done, or would have done, would cause permanent damage. I felt your rage. You were gathering for a death blow, Zenisa. If the council turns him over to you, you can do whatever you please, and you will have to live with the aftermath. But while he is in my custody, you will follow my rules."

"Alder, what is Solisa planning?" Zenisa asked, dismissing Suleima.

"How would I know the Great Goddess's plans?"

"So you are no longer her favorite pet?" Zenisa taunted, "Did you become weak? Is that why you were able to be trapped by this lowly shaman? Why you fell out of favor with my dear sister?"

Suleima's eyes connected with Gage's and Dynasira's. This was new information, surprising information.

"The Goddess has her reasons for her secrecy," he said.

"Because she knows even her most loyal followers would abandon her and her madness?" Zenisa continued, "Because no one would want that book opened, no one would want that book to even exist unless they had gone completely mad."

"You do not understand. You never have understood," he replied.

"Oh, but you do, Alder? You understand opening that book will bring about the end of this world as we know it. Will bring the fae and every other magical being to their knees. It is starting creation again. To take away weaknesses is to increase a being's power tenfold. If Solisa plans to do such a thing in her quest for creation of monstrosities, there is no telling how much damage she could do. With no weaknesses, how does anyone keep a being with so much power in check?"

Zenisa turned on her heel and walked back to solid ground. The three of them followed and the lake became liquid again. "Solisa is mad. There is no other explanation."

"She is your sister?" Dynasira interjected.

"Yes. I would rather not discuss this here. The Green Knight is secure for the time being. He cannot break free. We can return to your cabin, and then you may call your council if you must," Zenisa said, before turning and heading back the way they came.

Suleima sat on a fallen log at the edge of her property outside of her ward. She refused to invite the fae into her home. Gage sat next to her, his arm draped casually around her shoulder. Dynasira leaned against a nearby tree, and they waited for Zenisa to speak.

"Solisa is my twin," Zenisa began. "Our mother was a summer fae, our father from the winter fae. Generally, winter fae are considered cold and cruel to others, while the summer fae are thought of as sweet and unassuming. I retained the personality of my mother's people while having powers like my father. Solisa was the reverse. Father was not like most of the winter fae at that time, so where her cruelty came from was a mystery to us, even then.

"Solisa grew crueler as she aged. She may not have directly been their cause of death, but she had some involvement. Of that, I have no doubt.

"After their deaths, Solisa went off, gathering any fae who would worship and follow her. I stayed behind, in our family home, doing what I could to protect the fae who needed it. We have steered clear of each other for many centuries. She lives her way, far away from me, and I live mine. We have crossed paths very infrequently, and the encounters always end in violence.

"We do not agree on much, my sister and I, but the biggest hurdle we have is her desire for creation. Solisa experiments on creatures. Making hybrids of creatures, performing spells to make changes to their makeup. Physically tearing them to pieces and putting them back together. You name it, she has probably done it to some creature or another to satisfy her curiosity.

"If what you say is contained in the book she stole, in her hands, this world would be in great peril."

"You said The Green Knight was her 'pet.' What did you mean?" Dynasira asked.

"He did her bidding. No matter how violent, no matter how un-provoked, he did whatever she asked," Zenisa answered. "She called on him whenever she had something truly heinous on her agenda. He killed without mercy, simply to please her."

"What would have been her motivation to help someone like Kylin? She was a shaman, but as far as I know, she has no fae in her blood. She was a sickly child, a teenager when she would have passed," Suleima asked.

"Solisa would have seen her as an easy target. That young girl never had a chance. Not only would Solisa's teachings have twisted her, but the very magic used to create a vampire twists to evil. Solisa and Kylin would both have had to reach out and embrace the Void. It would have corrupted them and continued twisting them to this day."

"The Void?"

Suleima turned to him, looking at their clasped hands before beginning. "You remember on Mt. Lucent, when the Slyph appeared?" At Gage's nod, she continued, "I only had access to my air magic at that point, and it was useless. But, you were in danger. I needed to save you." She squeezed his hand, "Somehow, I felt a spark and reached for it. Aether. Remember?"

Gage nodded, "Unfortunately, I remember too much about our trip." He rubbed his thumb over a scar which had worsened because of his attack on her when under the influence of the Phoenix.

"Aether is pure magic, untold possibility. Void is the antithesis of that. Again, I don't know much about the Void, just as I knew very little about Aether. I do know Void is corrupt magic. Everything has a balance. Each element balances the next. Aether and Void are balances. Touching the Void should be as rare as touching Aether."

Zenisa continued, "Aether and Void are more difficult for shamans to touch. They are reliant on the elements of the world to replenish and provide their powers. Fae do not need those elements. While our powers tend to use an element, we do not rely on the earth to provide them. Our magic does use Aether or Void. While not easy to touch, it is the basis of our magics, where they come from. We are touching a small piece of it each time we use magic. But reaching out to the Void is forbidden."

"Was I able to touch Aether because of my fae magic?" Suleima asked.

"I do not believe that is why," Zenisa answered, "I have heard of the Trial of Mt. Lucent. It is a challenge I would never wish to take. Your fae magic had not manifested when you were a child, which is why your mother sent you with Erist. Fae children have their abilities from birth, or toddlerhood at the latest. I did not believe you would ever develop fae magic. Instead, I believe by doing what is impossible for a shaman and touching the Aether, it may have unlocked your dormant fae magic which would never have been realized otherwise."

There was silence for a while.

Zenisa broke it. "You still need more training, Suleima. I will not sacrifice another of my lesser fae for your teachings."

"I didn't ask you to," Suleima said, defensively.

"Patience, child," Zenisa said, holding up her hand. "I lay no blame for the loss of Zia at your feet. I see now how much she meant to you and your pack. However, since I will not send another lesser fae here, there is only one option. I will need to stay."

"Woah," Gage said, standing quickly, blocking Suleima from getting up, "This is our territory. We will not have you in here trying to take over." Dynasira, too, stood straight from where she had been leaning, not speaking, but backing Gage just the same.

"Peace, Alpha," Zenisa responded. "I would be here only in the capacity of a teacher. I will not be trying to run anything here. I will leave that to you and your council."

"Sul?" Dynasira said.

Suleima stood, winding around Gage so she could stand in front of Zenisa. "My property is outside the Amber Mountain Pack territory," she said, placing her hand on Gage's forearm to prevent the protest she knew was coming. "I will not allow you access to my home after today's display. I am aware my wards stand no chance against you, so I must have your word you will respect those boundaries."

"I can show you how to strengthen your wards with fae magic, so they cannot be torn down so easily," Zenisa offered.

Suleima nodded. "I would appreciate it."

"I noticed a rocky outcropping, similar to my own homestead, about one hundred yards west of here. Is that spot acceptable?" she asked. At Suleima's agreement, Zenisa said goodbye.

"I don't like this," Gage said as Zensia was out of hearing range.

Dynasira replied, "Neither do I. Which is why I'll be camping out here for the foreseeable future."

Gage nodded his appreciation. "I need to get back to the pack house to take care of some things. I'll be back later. Summon the council. Have them meet us out here."

"That will probably be best," Suleima agreed. "They can come to see The Green Knight and meet the Ice Goddess as well. We can also touch base to see if anyone found out anything about the key while we are at it."

Gage pulled her in for a kiss. "I don't like leaving you here with her or the knight. Stay safe."

"Thank you for trusting me," Suleima responded softly.

"It would never be you I didn't trust," he replied, then after a final kiss, headed for his truck.

Dynasira linked her arm with Suleima's. "Ooh, I need details!" She laughed, half dragging Suleima to the cabin.

Chapter 21

Suleima woke before dawn. Dynasira was still asleep outside, curled up in dragon form. Suleima dressed and mentally prepared for the day ahead. Punishments were her least favorite part of being on the council. Even knowing The Green Knight felt no remorse and would happily repeat his actions. And the fae could not be cut off from their magic.

Dawn was peeking over the horizon when she felt Gage and Kaly enter her territory. She walked out to find Dynasira shifting as she sensed their arrival too. Kaly stayed slightly behind Gage as they walked through the ward.

Gage swept over to her quickly, embracing her with a lingering kiss. Pressing his forehead to hers, he said, "I've missed you."

Kaly playfully elbowed Gage aside. "My turn," she said, giving Suleima a big hug. "I'm so happy he finally did it!" she whispered excitedly in Suleima's ear.

Gage cleared his throat, and Kaly laughed.

Suleima blushed and smiled back at her, "Me too."

Kaly began to rapid fire questions at Suleima about the last few days events, while Gage and Dynasira drifted a few feet away, talking in whispered tones. Suleima held up a hand to stop Kaly and stepped toward her mate and her best friend. "Why are we whispering?" she asked.

Gage reached out, pulling Suleima against his side, "Just making sure last night was uneventful."

"Everything was quiet," Suleima answered. "You can ask me."

"I know, but I wanted Dyna's take on it. You tend to sugarcoat things, so I won't worry."

"I wouldn't lie to you," Suleima responded, offended.

He turned her so they faced each other, his arms linked behind the small of her back, her long braid brushing at the tops of his hands. "You'd never lie. I know," he clarified, "But, you have been known to make it seem less serious than it was." He kissed the end of her nose. "I worry anytime we're apart."

Suleima nodded, before lifting her head to look over his shoulder.

Agron landed right outside of her ward, and Lysom was with him. Suleima altered the ward so they could pass without incident and waved them over. Before they reached the clearing where the rest of them stood, a messenger bird arrived from Hamanad.

Everyone was quiet as Suleima relayed the message. "Hamanad is too far to make it for this council meeting. He has a lead on the key, and he is headed that way instead. He says he does not believe he will be needed to break any tie in a vote regarding the punishment of The Green Knight, but can be reached by messenger, if it is needed."

Suleima, Dynasira, and Gage brought out chairs and benches from the house and porch, forming a circle in the center of the ward. Once everyone was seated, Suleima disclosed the details of the previous couple days to the council. "The Green Knight is still at the lake.

We will walk there as soon as we are finished here. You may ask any questions you may have of him, and then we can reach a decision as to his punishment." She went on to tell them about the appearance of the Ice Goddess and her plan to stay near Suleima for the time being.

"I don't like the idea of her being here," Lysom chimed in. "How do we know she hasn't gone to the lake to interfere with this green knight?"

"Because she gave her word she would not," Zenisa said from outside the ward.

Suleima interjected, "I know there is bias toward the fae. The incidents over the last weeks have done nothing to dissuade those notions. However, as the Ice Goddess and The Green Knight are in my territory, I take responsibility for them. I have asked the council here to decide his punishment. I will stand as the intermediary between this council and the Ice Goddess, if she does not agree with the punishment. She is here, not to deal with The Green Knight, but to help me to learn to control and harness the fae magic that has been unlocked within me."

"And if we should decide to cut him off from his magic as punishment?" Agron asked.

"As it is fae magic, we would need her assistance," Suleima answered.

"And if she refuses?" Lysom continued.

Suleima held her hand up as Zenisa opened her mouth to speak. When Zenisa stayed quiet—to Suleima's surprise—she said, "The Ice Goddess is very much in favor of death for The Green Knight. She was ready to end him yesterday. If it is the will of the council, I believe she will assist us in whatever we need her to."

Suleima stood, followed by the rest of the council.

All too soon, the entire council, minus Hamanad stood in the clearing, staring at The Green Knight. True to her word, Zenisa had not harmed him through the night. Suleima took a steadying breath and stepped forward, "Anyone who wants to pose a question, please step forward." She turned to Zenisa, "Would you re-freeze the ice around him, so we can approach more easily?"

Lysom was the first to speak, "Why were you sent here?"

The Green Knight stayed quiet.

"Who sent you?" Agron asked.

Silence.

"Do you feel any remorse for the actions you have taken? The life you have taken?" Lysom asked, impatience evident in his tone.

Continued silence.

"Do you have nothing to say to defend yourself against these claims?" Agron continued.

"Pardon my interruption," Zenisa said, cautiously approaching again. "I can make him speak, if you wish."

Suleima stepped forward. "We will not force him to defend himself."

"You lowly beings have no authority over me. Why should I waste my breath?" he said, mockingly.

"Considering one of these lowly beings managed to cage you, Alder, I would suggest putting a damper on your arrogance," Zenisa replied.

"My mistress will send someone for me," Alder said confidently. "I have nothing to fear from any of you."

Suleima raised her brow, "You have been trapped here for the better part of two days. I should think your mistress would have come for you by now, if she was going to come."

"I know my sister," Zenisa said. "If she was going to come back for you, it is only to shut you up permanently, so you would not spill any more of her secrets."

"I do not *know* her secrets!" Alder shouted.

"Then you are of no use to me," Zenisa said dismissively.

"I vote we turn him over to Zenisa. Let her do what she wishes with him."

Gage's startled expression matched those on the other council members, but he quickly masked it. "I agree."

"As do I," said Kaly.

The others indicated their agreement as well.

"It is unanimous, Zenisa," Suleima said. "I turn him over to you."

"No!" he shouted. "Do not turn me over to *her*!"

"Give us a reason to reconsider," Suleima said flatly.

"I do not know her plan. I only know she searches for a key for a book. I have no idea what is in the book, or why it requires a key. I truly do not know anything more!" he responded.

Gage stepped forward, "Why is she targeting Suleima?"

"Solisa feels no personal threat from Suleima. She has repeatedly said this, but she does believe Suleima could delay her plans. Dirrin was a pawn, a means to an end. If Suleima had not killed Dirrin, Solisa would have, the moment she knew he kept the knowledge of the book from her."

Zenisa turned to Suleima. "Solisa is not aware of your"—she glanced at The Green Knight—"background. At least not that I know of. Would Kylin have known?"

Suleima shook her head. "I knew nothing of it until before coming to find you. Erist kept it a secret from me and everyone else."

Suleima asked, "Dirrin was working with Solisa?"

"He desired to rule over all. Solisa saw this as an opportunity. Dirrin could kill off whoever he wanted, clear the way for her to take his place after he did the hard work."

Suleima turned to the rest of the council. "What is the vote of the council now?"

"I vote he be cut off from his magic," Gage said, "He killed a pack member and threatened my mate."

"I second," Kaly piped up, "No one comes at the pack without consequences."

Suleima turned to Dynasira, "The compound where the remaining prisoners are, is there any way for it to hold a fae and contain its magic?"

Dynasira shook her head. "We can't cut them off from their magic the same way we can for a shaman."

"There is no way to make him safe without cutting off his magic," Lysom added, "and he has shown no remorse for his actions."

"I agree," Agron said, stepping forward, "Had he shown any remorse, we may have been able to work toward some other solution. But as it stands, he must be neutralized."

Suleima nodded. "Alder, The Green Knight, our council has come to a unanimous decision. For your crimes, the unprovoked attack on our territory, and the murder of a pack member, we hereby sentence you to a dissolution of your magic." Her voice cracked with emotion. "Your death as a result of this punishment is yet another tragic loss which never needed to be."

Gage took her by the hand. "So say us all."

"So say us all," echoed the rest of the council.

Gage turned to walk Suleima out of the clearing. "You don't need to be witness to this punishment. It will be done and the others will make sure it is humane," Gage said.

"I should face the consequences of my choices."

"Not today, Sul. Today, I am giving you a break from the punishment you seem to feel you need." Gage said.

"Actions have consequences. If I take an action, I must see it through, even to unpleasant results," she responded.

Gage kissed her on her forehead, "And that is one of the many reasons I love you. And one of the reasons I am protecting you from yourself. Give yourself grace."

Suleima closed her eyes for a moment before opening them to peer deeply into his, "I love you, too, Mate." She leaned into him, taking his lips with hers, holding on like he was her lifeline. He held her just as tightly, pulling away a few moments later, both of them breathing heavily, she touched her forehead to his and closed her eyes, breathing him in and relishing their closeness, until their breathing slowed.

Suleima looked up. "Well, I will be damned."

Chapter 22

GAGE AND SULEIMA STOOD facing the rocky outcropping Zenisa made her temporary home, while she was in Amber Mountain. It was like they had been transported to the mountain where she lived. Her home, like the one they found her in, was nestled into the rock face. Suleima would bet, if they entered her house, it would look the same as it did when they visited her the first time. The front of the home blended into the rock face, so unless you knew what you were looking for, or had seen it before, it was nearly invisible.

"I probably don't want to think about how much power it took to recreate that," Gage said, staring ahead.

Suleima nodded, agreeing wholeheartedly. "That's an intimidating sight."

"It's supposed to be." Zenisa's voice came from behind them.

Gage growled and spun, keeping Suleima behind him.

Zenisa put up her hands. "It was not my intention to startle you, Alpha." She shifted her gaze to Suleima. "It is done."

Suleima took a steadying breath and nodded her head once. "Thank you for your help."

"I would give you today to rest, but I fear my sister will not wait much longer. We should start your training," Zenisa said.

Suleima stepped around Gage. "I am ready."

Zenisa led them into the woods, away from the lake. "Show me what you have been able to do so far."

"Most things I've done so far have been accidental. I have had better luck combining my shamanistic magic with the fae magic," Suleima replied, then continued to tell her about the cyclone she was able to produce to drive Kylin away.

Zenisa's eyebrows rose as the story unfolded. "Your magics combined?"

"Well, I used my shamanistic magic to help to mold my fae magic."

"Show me," Zenisa said.

Gage stepped back, giving her room. Suleima closed her eyes and found the cool, fluid feeling. Remembering what Zia said, she didn't reach for it, just let it flow. She opened her eyes and two small jets of water bounced upwards in each of her palms. She smiled. Then she changed her focus and pushed at the jets of water, launching them at nearby trees.

"Nice job," Zenisa said. "On Zia's last visit to me, she said she saw you throw waves of water at another shaman. Can you recreate that?"

"I don't know," Suleima said. "She was threatening Zia, and Gage was in the firing line. I have only been able to do things like that when I'm protecting someone."

Zenisa's expression changed.

"I told Zia, and I am telling you. You will not put my friends in danger to make me learn. Either I will learn without, or I will not learn. Am I clear?"

"Yes," Zenisa replied and pointed to a nearby tree. "Send a wave of water like you did before. Aim for that tree."

Suleima tried to remember what she had done and how she was feeling when she sent the waves at Xiala. Nothing happened.

Gage touched the spot between her brows. "Don't try so hard," he whispered.

Suleima relaxed, starting at the top of her head and working her way down, then she guided the magic, beginning in her toes, waving up through her body, and pushed out from her shoulders. A wave of water rushed forward. It didn't make it to the tree, but she did make the wave. She turned her huge grin at Gage, "Thank you."

"Again," Zenisa prompted.

Suleima repeated the action and this time the wave went a bit further, still not reaching the tree, but closer.

"Can you picture someone at the tree? The tree is Kylin, or the person you originally targeted with the wave."

Suleima stretched her neck and concentrated on the tree, rather than the magic. This time, the wave washed into the base of the tree.

"What did you do there? Can you explain it to me?" Zenisa asked.

"That time, I focused on the tree, not the magic."

"Let's try something new. Can you combine your shamanistic magic with it?"

Suleima rolled her shoulders and turned back to the tree. She allowed the magic to drift from her toes and up, guiding the wave as she had done before, and this time pushed with her air magic. The wave hit the tree high up, with force, shaking the upper branches.

It was late afternoon by the time she and Gage arrived back at her cabin. Suleima and Gage sat on the porch watching the sky slowly darken.

"What happens now?" she asked into the deepening dark.

"We stay vigilant for Kylin to return, but we wait for news of the key from Hamanad," he replied.

She snuggled in closer, drawn to his warmth, "If Solisa gets the key first..."

Gage pulled her onto his lap, wrapping her in his arms, "Then we will deal with it. But don't borrow trouble," he said, "Just enjoy the quiet evening." He pressed his lips to hers. Gage pulled away with a growl at the approach of footsteps from behind the house.

"It is Zenisa," Suleima said, standing up and walking off of the porch.

"She has done enough training for the day," Gage growled.

"I agree, Alpha. But I said I would help her to reinforce her wards with fae magic, so neither I nor another fae could pull them down so easily. I intend to do it this evening, so you are both protected."

When Gage would have growled again at the implication he may not be enough protection, Suleima said, "Thank you, Zenisa." She paused a moment. "If Kylin comes by, could she pull the ward down like she did before?"

Zenisa thought for a moment before she spoke, "Could she? Yes."

"So what is the point of putting up a new ward?" Gage asked.

"As an energy vampire, she absorbs the energy of someone or something to power her own magic. With fae magic in it, there is a risk it will, in fact, give her a boost." Zenisa held her hand up as Gage began to protest. She directed her attention fully to Suleima, dismissing Gage. "But you said when she pulled down your ward before she continued to drain you, because your power and the ward are connected, correct?"

"Yes. She drained my magic through the ward.""With fae magic in it, Solisa and I, or any other fae, would have difficulty breaking through, because you will mix it with your shamanistic magic. The fae magic will allow you to tie off your shamanistic magic, so Kylin could not drain you at the same time."

"And I can alter any ward this way?"

"Yes," Zenisa answered.

Suleima turned to Gage, "After we finish with this ward, we can go to the pack house, and I can redo that one as well."

"One thing at a time." He kissed the end of her nose.

"Watch me first," Zenisa said, "I will try to slow down to show you how I do it. We may need to try several times, since you will be weaving your shamanistic magic with your fae magic. That should make it harder for *anyone* to breach it."

Suleima reached out with her senses to feel how Zenisa manipulated her magic to form a small ward outside of her own. When it was in place, a small dome over a flowering bush, Suleima reached forward, trying to pick one of the flowers. Her hand stopped at the edge of the dome, and she felt an ever-increasing jolt as she tried to pass her hand through the dome.

Gage growled. "Please, stop."

Suleima looked back at him, pulling her hand back. His eyes were a bright violet, and his jaw clenched as if he was holding back his shift. "I can feel your pain. Please, stop."

She nodded and knelt, burying her hand as she usually did. She pictured the magic she felt while Zenisa was creating her ward, closed her eyes, and tried to emulate it, weaving it into her current ward, creating as seamless a pattern as she could manage. When she finished, she stood back.

Zenisa approached the large ward and reached out her hand.

Gage placed his hand on the small of her back, ready to support her.

Suleima felt it when Zenisa touched it. The burn began almost immediately, and she braced herself for the coming onslaught, but it was not draining her further. The fae magic was stopping the ward from pulling more energy from her. And it was holding.

Zenisa pushed more power into the ward and twisted her hand. Suleima closed her eyes against the pain, but the ward held. Another push from Zenisa, and Gage growled. Suleima opened her eyes then and pushed back hard. Zenisa's hand yanked away from the ward, smiling.

"Good job. I wondered how long it would take you to figure out you can make your ward fight back," Zenisa praised.

Gage's grumble told them both what he thought of that test.

The next morning, Suleima woke with the dawn and stretched, smiling to find Gage still fast asleep beside her. She watched him sleep for a moment, studying his face in this relaxed and vulnerable state. Suleima always felt protective of him, but now there was a primal nature to it. She would move heaven and earth to get to him, to protect him. It was a scary feeling, to care so much about someone.

Gage's eye opened and met hers. There was violet around the rim of his irises, even now when he wasn't using any power. "What are you smiling about?" he asked, "What are you thinking?"

"I got your bite mark to show I am your mate," she began, "You share my eye color. I can see the violet in your eyes, even now. It enhances the icy blue from before."

Gage reached out, pulling her into his embrace. "I'm proud to carry your mark. I am yours, and you are *mine*."Soon after, they met Zenisa on the path.

Suleima used her senses to reach out ahead of them, making sure the way was clear. The warmth of her hand in Gage's provided a calmness and security she craved in this uncertain time. She could never properly define how much he meant to her with words alone.

Without thinking, she had led them to the clearing by the lake, and she stopped short when the lake came into view. There was no evidence of what had taken place the day before. In her mind's eye, she could see The Green Knight still standing in the lake, but the pristine water and surrounding shoreline showed no evidence of it being disturbed. It was as if the whole event had been erased.

"I did my best to put everything back as it had been," Zenisa said. "Dynasira helped since I never saw this place before the fight occurred."

Suleima found it difficult to speak around the lump in her throat, so she simply nodded. Gage's simple "Thank you," would have to do.

Suleima's gaze floated to the tree Zia had hit and fallen. Tears welled up in her eyes, and Gage's tightening hand, as he followed her gaze nearly undid her. At the base of the tree, a beautiful bush of moon flowers grew. The bush was fully grown, and it had not been there the day before.

Zenisa followed their gazes. "Zia loved moon flowers. I wanted to make sure a piece of her stayed here with you, her pack."

After a full day of training, Suleima was exhausted but invigorated. She was getting better, more consistent. Her magics were blending. Anytime she reached for water magic, they both came to her call.

Gage and Suleima went back to her cabin, enjoying a quiet meal before heading to the pack house. She wanted to reinforce the ward around the house, and Gage needed to check in with the rest of the pack.

Suleima was surprised to find most of the pack at the house when she arrived. She pulled her truck in behind Gage's, climbed out, and met him at the tailgate of his truck.

"They're here because they heard I've taken a mate."

Suleima dropped her chin, her cheeks reddening. She hated being the center of attention.

Enveloping both of her hands in one of his, Gage used his other hand to tilt her chin back up, forcing her to look at him. "They knew who you were to me when I left to go with you to Mount Lucent."

Her eyebrows rose in surprise.

"Let's go," he said, dropping a quick kiss to her lips. "They want to greet their Alpha's mate. You can work on the wards after."

She was overwhelmed by the number of wolves she met that day and, after reinforcing the ward around the pack house, Suleima excused herself to return to her cabin. She needed to recharge and re-center herself, so she left Gage and the pack and drove her old truck back home.

Chapter 23

Sulemia jumped from her bed and scrambled to throw on clothes and shoes. She grabbed her bow and arrows and bolted into the yard, screaming for Dynasira. She sprinted for her truck, pulling at her earth magic as she ran, increasing her speed. She sensed Dynasira stirring in the distance, but she wasn't moving fast enough. Suleima jumped in her rusty, old truck and pushed that truck to its limits as she raced down the mountain road as quickly as she dared.

She skidded to a halt as she approached the ward at the pack house, or where it was supposed to be, tires spitting gravel. As she jumped out of the car, Dynasira landed beside her and immediately shifted.

"What happened?" Dynasira asked.

"The ward was pulled down. It must have been Kylin. The energy was just sucked out of it," Suleima scanned the area, but found no trace of Kylin with her senses... and Gage was missing too. She sensed a few other wolves in the pack house, but none moved. In an instant, Suleima's feet pounded the ground as she closed the distance to the main house. She yelled for Dynasira to check for signs of Kylin from above as she ran, not stopping until she reached the porch.

The front door of the pack house was wide open. She heard the television in the back room blaring. She raced from room to room, until she found one of the wolves. He was asleep, but she couldn't rouse him. She first tried to talk to him to wake him, not wanting to surprise him. Then she tried shaking him. His breathing was steady and strong, but he never stirred.

She repeated this with every pack member she found. Nothing seemed to rouse them. Suleima ran back out of the house and yelled for Dynsira, who landed a few moments later. "Did you see anything?" As Dynasira shook her head, she continued, "Get Zenisa. I can't wake anyone inside. They have to be under some sort of fae spell, and I don't know how to unlock it."

She ran back inside as soon as Dynasira was in the air and headed for Kaly. Suleima sat gently on the edge of the bed and closed her eyes, opening her senses, tried to look with her magic. When she opened her eyes again, feeling out with her senses, a cloud surrounded Kaly and the other pack members in the house. She placed a hand on the surface of the cloud. The warmth of the air was now noticeable. She tilted her head, her brow furrowed as she tried to grasp it. It felt like a bubble. She pressed down through it to touch Kaly, but the cloud was still a thin barrier between them.

On the verge of panic, Suleima concentrated on her breathing. She could not afford to miss a single detail or make a rash move that would hurt one of the wolves.

Afraid to probe the spell without knowing what she was dealing with, Suleima stood and walked down the hallway to the room she was sure was Gage's. He was missing. She knew that already from their mate bond.

Her senses still open, she entered the room. A haze hovered inside. She reached out and felt another barrier, similar to the one around the pack members, but this one felt sticky to the touch.

Suleima tried calling fae water magic; it pinged off of the barrier and landed in the hallway behind her. She tried her shamanistic power over water, and the barrier shivered and shied away from her. She was about to try to use her earth magic against it when she heard Dynasira and Zenisa enter the pack house.

Suleima met them at the top of the stairs.

"This magic is fae, but it is strange," Zenisa said.

"Can we break it without harming them?"

"I don't know. Something else is woven here…" Zenisa trailed off, leaving Kaly's room and heading to another. "I can feel this spell deteriorate as we stand here. It should dissipate on its own, but I have no idea how long it will take."

Suleima led Zenisa to Gage's room. "And this?" She tried to keep the panic from her voice. "Can we break this one?"

She raised her eyebrows at Suleima's tone, but Zenisa stood at the door and reached in. "This is a powerful barrier. It hides what is inside. What we see is not what is."

"My fae magic bounced off of it. It doesn't like my shamanistic magic. It seemed to recoil from it."

"Show me."

Suleima called water again with her fae magic but used her shamanistic magic to mold and move it.

This time, Zenisa also watched the barrier shiver and recoil. "Try using earth against it."

The earth magic bounced off as well.

Zenisa motioned for Dynasira to step back and formed a long, sharp shard of ice. She guided it into place where the water had hit the barrier. "Ice is nothing but frozen water. Use your magic to manipulate mine. Shove it into the barrier when I tell you." She backed up three paces and erected her own shield in front of the door of the room.

"How bad will the blowback be?" Dynasira asked.

"I honestly don't know," Zenisa replied.

"Make the shield bigger. No one in this house gets hurt. Not us, and *not my pack*."

Zenisa nodded, and as soon as that was done, Suleima shoved with all of her strength.

A whoosh of air blew their hair back, like the popping of an enormous balloon. Gage's room no longer looked ordinary. A dresser had toppled to the floor, with gouge marks marring its top and sides. A lamp lay shattered next to the bed, and blood marred the white marble shards from the lamp base.

Suleima's knees buckled.

Dynasira approached her, placing a hand on her shoulder. "This isn't Gage's blood. It smells like..."

"Kylin," Suleima and Dynasira said together.

"We should wake the pack."

Suleima walked straight to Kaly's room. She called each of the elements but to no avail. Frustration threatened to overtake her; her knees threatened to crumble beneath her. But she couldn't fall apart now. She needed to keep it together, to figure out how to find and rescue Gage.

Suleima looked at Zenisa. "My magic had no effect. How can we break this?"

Zenisa approached Kaly and placed her hand above the magic surrounding her. "I feel the heat of the magic Kylin used, but it is not alone. Something else is weaved in with her spell and I can't put my finger on what it is."

"If you break it with force…" Dynasira began.

"It could kill them," Zenisa finished. "The blowback might be minor, but it may also be fatal. Until I am sure what else is woven in here, I would not advise using force."

"I need to find Gage. I can't wait. Kylin could easily kill him if she wanted. I need to get to him before she does," Suleima's hands balled up into fists as she spoke.

"How is waking the pack going to help you find him?"

"Not the pack. I want them out of this spell and out of danger, but to find Gage, I need Kaly. She and Gage have a special connection. She can communicate with him over long distances, and she can communicate with him when he is in wolf form."

"How do you know Kylin hasn't killed him yet?"

"I can feel it."

Zenisa reached for Suleima's hand. "Close your eyes and take a deep breath to steady yourself."

Suleima did as she was instructed, though she just wanted to scream.

"Better," Zenisa said, "Now, I need you to focus on the feeling that tells you that Gage is still alive. You are the mate of the Alpha. Kaly may have a strong connection to the Alpha, but it pales in comparison to the mate bond. Close your eyes and tune out everything but him. Feel for that glimmer that tells you he is alive. Reach for that feeling." Zenisa's voice had become soft and melodic.

Suleima's mind drifted to that moment in her house when Gage encouraged her to use her fae magic. As she did then, Suleima concentrated on relaxing her muscles, letting her mind wander to where she needed to focus. Suleima shivered. "It's cold."

Dynsira grabbed a blanket and brought it to Suleima.

"No, it is cold where Gage is," she clarified but grabbed the blanket anyway. His scent on the blanket was strong and she brought it to her nose.

"Is there light?" Zenisa asked.

"No. Or, not much. He's shifted. He is in a cage of some kind." She reached deeper, trying to find something more. "The floor is soil and rock."

Dynasira spoke softly. "Are you seeing what he is seeing? Feeling what he is feeling?"

"I think so," she answered, "Everything is in shades of gray and I can see the tops of his front paws. I can smell the dirt."

"Can you feel the dirt and soil? Does it call to you?"

Suleima pushed at the dirt under Gage's paw. Gage moved it and she noticed the small plant sprout that had appeared where his paw had been.

"Concentrate on one message you want to send to him. Block out everything else," Zenisa said. "His location, his physical health, encouragement... whatever. Just focus on one thing and try to get it through to him."

"He's warning me away," she said, smiling.

"Did he forget who you are?" Dynasira laughed.

"Must have." She quieted her mind again, searching for more. "It's very loud. Deafeningly so."

"Loud and cold, dirt and rocks," Dynasira listed, "Anything else? That's very vague."

"Wait..." She opened her senses further. "Kylin is there." Gage snarled and backed away from the edge of the cage as Kylin reached her hand inside. "She's wet." Suleima added. I can see the water dripping and steaming from her shirt sleeve.

"Near water that is loud, a floor of dirt and rocks and dim lighting... Is there a raging river near here? He's only been gone for a half hour or so, they can't have gone far," Zenisa stated.

"Not a river," Suleima began.

"The Falls," Dynasira finished.

Chapter 24

SULEIMA GATHERED A FEW supplies from Gage's room into an old pack of his, then her bow and arrows from the floor of Kaly's room, where she had left them and headed down the stairs. "Zenisa, would you stay with my pack? Keep them safe?"

"I could come with you and help."

"I need my pack safe. You are the only one I know powerful enough to protect them all on your own. If someone comes here to harm them further, it will be a fae."

Zenisa nodded.

"Thank you."

Dynasira walked out onto the porch with Suleima, "If you think I'm staying behind..."

"Nope." Suleima smiled. "You're my ride."

***

After a short flight, they crept through the woods, winding their way closer and closer to the falls.

Suleima continued to scan the area, but she couldn't find Kylin. Something seemed off, about a hundred yards east of where she and Dynasira stood. Something was out there. Not Kylin, but something. Dynasira went into the air, to see what Suleima sensed.

The moment they split up, Suleima sensed Kylin. She was nearby, directly in the path Suleima was headed. Suleima walked carefully, keeping as quiet as possible despite the sounds of the waterfall.

She concentrated on a tree. Pulling with her earth magic, Suleima manipulated the root system of the tree, raising up one of the roots several inches higher off the ground. She pulled at a vine that had tangled into the tree branches, elongating it, causing a loop to dangle lower. She kept a hold on the vine and waited.

When Kylin passed, she stumbled slightly over the root and into the looped vine. Suleima snatched the vine, twisting and twirling it, locking Kylin in place. She only had a moment before Kylin sucked the energy and life from the vine and broke through the now brittle husk.

Suleima blasted dirt and air into Kylin's face, trying to keep her disoriented, and pulled up a shield using both her fae and shamanistic water magic. She sent a water spear next, hitting Kylin in the shoulder and piercing her flesh.

Kylin let out a screech of frustration, and her arms lit, the intensity of the blaze, temporarily blinding. A fireball slammed into Suleima's shield, and the hissing sound it made temporarily drowned out the cacophony of the waterfall, but the shield held. She forced more power and water into her shield while putting the large trunk of a tree between her and Kylin.

Suleima heard the Dynasira screech, but she tried to block it out, focusing on the threat in front of her. She felt Gage below her, slamming his body against the bars of the cage.

Suleima felt the heat at her back as a fireball slammed into the trunk of the tree she used for cover. She dove away from the now smoldering tree, intent on liquifying the ground to trap Kylin. But the howl she felt more than heard from Gage distracted her. She recovered quickly enough to roll out of the way of the next fireball which shot burning leaves into the air, raining down around her. Continuing to roll, she managed to get herself behind another wide tree trunk and back on her feet. She took a moment to try to convey serenity through their bond before turning back to the fight at hand, the thing she *should* be concentrating on.

Suleima shot dirt and air up into Kylin's face and followed it with another spear of water. Kylin screamed again and blasted the tree in front of Suleima with a fireball, igniting it. She splashed water at the tree, dampening the flames, and tracked Kylin to her new position, dodging the next fireball she loosed. This time, after erupting the dirt into Kylin's face, Suleima fired an arrow from her bow. The new set of arrows that Gage had given her was metal, so Kylin couldn't just burn it out.

She sent two more quick bursts of water at Kylin, before moving to a different spot which offered her more cover. She took a moment to reach out her senses and felt Dynasira approaching fast, with something on her heels. Whatever it was, it would soon be in her line of sight.

The distraction was enough for Kylin to fire several fireballs in quick succession. Suleima's shield took two of those blasts, the third made it through, scorching the leather of Suleima's coat. She smothered the flames by pulling the air away from her arm, nocking and firing another arrow into the air. Using her air, she pulled the arrow in a different direction, striking Kylin in the arm, piercing through her arm and into her chest, pinning the arm just above the elbow.

Dynasira landed hard beside her, panting hard. "Incoming!"

Just as she spoke, a nightmarish creature emerged. A nuckelavee.

Only having read about them in books, Suleima was not prepared for the sight it presented. A creature that resembled a one-eyed horse, with the top half of a man emerging from the middle of its back. The nuckelavee had no skin, just bone and sinew. Its arms, from the man-like body, dragged along the ground as it ran using the legs of the horse. She fired an arrow as she and Dynasira backed away from it. Kylin took that opportunity to fire one last ball of flames at Suleima before disappearing from sight.

The nuckelavee reared back, its neigh more like a scream, and so high-pitched that Suleima and Dynasira both covered their ears. When it next opened its mouth, a brackish smoke emerged.

"Don't let that smoke touch you!" Dynasira shouted. "It's some kind of toxin or poison." She held out her hand in front of Suleima, who now saw the blackened and bubbling skin from her hand up through the middle of her forearm.

Suleima stirred the wind, pushing the air back toward the nuckelavee. It stomped its odd, fin-like hoof and lowered its horse head, the single, blood-red eye locked on them. The sickeningly green hair of the horse-like mane and on the man-like head waved with every movement. Its scream pierced the air as it charged them.

Dynasira shifted, lifting Suleima into the air with her in a single movement. When she noticed the odd listing of Dynasira's flight, Suleima looked up, and the scales of one of her wings was blackened, like her skin had been. After shooting boiling water at the nuckelavee, she landed hard again, behind the nuckelavee and shifted back. Sweat beaded on her forehead.

Suleima turned, grabbed Dynasira's unharmed hand, and ran, pulling her friend behind her. She remembered one thing about the nuckelavee. If she and Dynasira could get across the river, the nuckelavee couldn't follow. It abhorred fresh water. It could not cross it. She would be able to regroup, make a plan, and heal Dynasira.

When Dynasira stumbled, Suleima turned and fired two more arrows in quick succession. One hit its mark, lodging in the front flank of the nuckelavee, causing it to stumble and hampering its speed. She helped Dynasira to her feet. "Shift! Get across the river. I'll meet you there! Don't argue, just go!"

Suleima fired another arrow and turned in time to see Dynasira take off. She started running again, pulling at the earth to increase her speed. She used her earth magic to put barriers and trip hazards behind her, to slow the nuckelavee down. Turning, she fired another arrow this one hitting the man-like appendage in the abdomen when the nuckelavee lowered its horse-like head.

Even slowed down by the injuries and obstacles, the four-legged creature was quickly gaining on her. The river was close, only a few hundred feet away, but she wouldn't make it across before the nuckelavee caught up to her. She stopped and dropped to her knees and quickly created a ward around her body, like Zenisa had shown her. The nuckelavee pounded at the ward with its front hooves, sending sparks into the air, its screams of frustration piercing. Suleima blocked out the sound to the best of her ability and tied off the ward.

Closing her eyes, Suleima focused on the water. Using her combined magic, she gathered the water. Its rushing toward the the waterfall below was extremely difficult to fight against. Exhaustion pulled at her body, and sweat was running down her face, but she grit her teeth and soldiered on. She needed to help Dynasira. She needed to get to Gage.

She pushed up with earth and shoved forward with air. Her body pitched forward with the effort. A tidal wave of water careened out of the riverbed in her direction. Once it began moving, momentum took over, and Suleima pressed to the ground hoping that the ward would hold against the coming onslaught.

Chapter 25

The nuckelavee's screech, as the water engulfed the creature, was a thing of nightmares. Suleima felt the pressure as the water shoved against the ward, but it rolled right over.

Dynasira landed heavily next to her and shifted again. Her good hand bounced off the ward when she reached for Suleima.

Suleima took down the ward and looked up at her friend. "Sit down with me a moment," she said, patting the ground next to her. "Give me your injured arm."

Dynasira complied. "You have the energy left to try to heal this?"

"I can feel it spreading. It needs to be dealt with now," Suleima probed the wound carefully. "It's still mainly on the surface." Suleima followed her instincts. She gathered the water left behind in the soil from the wave. She molded the water, wrapping it like a sleeve around Dynasira's upper arm, and slowly pulled it down toward the affected area of her forearm and hand. Dynasira hissed at the pain but kept still as Suleima continued.

The affected area shrunk, the poison retreating from the fresh water as the nuckelavee would have. But, it stopped at her hand. Suleima pulled the water sleeve back up her arm and the poison began to re-take Dynasira's flesh, climbing back the way it had retreated. Sighing, Suleima pulled the water sleeve back down Dynasira's arm and left it like a cuff along her wrist.

"We will talk with Zenisa. If she cannot rid you of the poison herself, we can reach out to the jinn and their healers. For now, this should hold."

They each stood. Suleima's knees threatened to buckle, but she stiffened her resolve and, taking a deep breath, hiked toward the waterfall. She scanned with her senses the whole way, watching for the return of either Kylin or the nuckelavee. She hoped that the force of the water was enough to at least keep the nuckelavee away for a while if it didn't kill it. Once out of the path of the wave, the ground was much drier and easier to navigate. The effort it took to slog through the mud was taxing what little energy remained for Suleima.

Suleima found a rough path as they approached the cliff of the waterfall. It was only wide enough for one of them at a time, so single file, they cautiously picked their way down the path. The sound was so loud, there was no way to talk and be heard, but keeping their feet under them took all of their concentration anyway. Loose dirt and stones caused each of them to slip several times. Her grip on a stone along the wall of the path was the only thing that saved Suleima from a deadly plunge down the cliff.

About halfway down, a switchback led them back toward the waterfall. They skidded down the steep incline, and near the base of the waterfall, the path disappeared behind it. Hugging the wall, they managed to stay mostly dry. The path became slightly wider the further they got under the waterfall. Just past the midway point, a cave mouth opened.

Suleima sensed Gage inside. Very dim lighting illuminated deep in the cave, but the light was not strong enough to reach the entrance. There was a section of pitch-blackness between her and her mate. Suleima reached out, feeling for any sort of magic, delicately combing over the darkest areas. Although she couldn't feel anything off, she approached the cave and entered with extreme caution, constantly scanning for any surprises.

Ten feet into the cave, Suleima and Dynasira reached the section of the pitch. Sliding her feet along the floor to avoid missteps, she inched her way forward. Her toe hit an obstacle and a loud snap echoed along the walls. That sound was unmistakable: a steel hunter's trap. She had to give Kylin credit. Suleima would have never thought she would use a trap with no magic. It would be the perfect way to harm a magic user who couldn't scan for something ordinary or non-magical.

She sent tranquility through the bond to Gage through their connection, to let him know they were okay, and continued to pick her way through the pitch-black section of the cave. Although she couldn't see it, Suleima could feel the cave walls narrowing. The dim light, still out of reach, Suleima reached out her left hand to feel the cave wall.

Instant numbness was her first thought before her knees nearly buckled, but the steel jaws locked around her now-broken wrist would not let her sink that low.

Tears welled up in her eyes as she tried to breathe through the intense pain that began as soon as the initial shock wore off. Dynasira attempted to pull at the sides of the jaws, but with her injured hand, the attempts were futile.

Suleima did her best to block out the pain and felt through the cave with her senses. There was a tree growing on the other side of the cliff, near the cave. Its deep root system came close to the cave wall. Gritting her teeth, Suleima pulled at the root with earth, extending it into the cave. It was slow going; her concentration split in too many directions and her power low after the fights with Kylin and the nuckelavee.

After a few minutes, with sweat pouring off her face, the root was through the wall and thick enough to be of use. She waited for Dynasira to find and break off the root, bracing herself as Dynasira jammed the root into the mouth of the steel trap.

Dynasira started to put pressure on the root to pry open the jaws but stopped at Suleima's scream of pain. Gage threw himself against the cage.

Suleima placed her hand on Dynasira's shoulder. "Let me try something," she shouted, trying to be heard above the rushing water outside the cave. Suleima set her concentration back on the root that was still jammed in the jaws of the trap. Painstakingly, she was able to expand the width of the root. The jaws releasing seemed more painful than being clamped inside. As soon as she was free, Suleima dropped to her knees, panting.

Cradling her left arm against her body, she shook her head to clear the spots from her vision and stood gingerly. Only another ten or so feet until they were in the dimly lit portion of the cave. She could hear Gage's whimper now. He must be feeling her pain. She tried her best to block the pain from him and continued picking her way carefully, avoiding touching the walls this time.

Her toe set off one more trap as she slid her foot along the floor. She entered the domed area of the interior of the cave. A small glowing orb hovered in the far corner, creating the dim light. Stopping, she scanned the room with her senses to find any magical traps, but again came up empty. The only trace of magic was surrounding the cage.

She knelt next to it without touching it. "Dyna, keep watch on that tunnel we just came through." She needed to get Gage and leave as quickly as they could. Kylin would not be down for long.

As quickly as she could with only one hand, Suleima pulled ingredients from her pack and refilled her elemental magic. After the fight with Kylin and the nuckelavee, she was drained, but she consciously pulled only a small amount of each element. Pulling enough to refill her wells would leave her nearly unconscious and they were far from safe out here. She could rest when they returned to the pack house and refill fully there.

So much had happened, and the day wasn't anywhere near over.

She probed the spell around the cage. This spell was similar to the one that kept them out of Gage's room at the pack house. It was made from something different. This one recoiled from her earth magic, not her water. She closed her eyes and attempted to stir the dirt and rocks inside the cage. The spell didn't keep her magic out. She shook her head, and absently said, "Should have known I could do that. I was able to move dirt from the pack house." She looked at Gage, "I'm going to build a shield around you with dirt. Stay still in there. I'm going to try to break the spell around the cage, and hopefully the cage."

She rolled her right shoulder and stretched her neck. She reached for her earth magic first, building up a shell surrounding Gage. "Dyna," she said, "come over here and stand behind me."

As soon as Dynasira was in place, Suleima built up a shield around the two of them as well. That done, she placed her focus on the shield surrounding Gage, tying it off from herself. Attempting something like this next step was foreign to her, but she couldn't allow Gage to continue to be locked up. All of the work and practice with the fae magic and how to work it within her shamanistic magic gave her the courage to be brave and try something new.

This time, she formed a second shield around Gage, this one between her original shield and the cage. Pushing more dirt and rock into the second shield, she slowly increased its size. It soon pushed against the spell trapping him in there. She paused a moment to clear her mind and sharpen her focus. "Brace yourself," she told Dynasira. "This may backfire." Suleima restarted, pushing more and more dirt and rock into the second shield. The more she pushed, the more the caging spell fought back but she continued to increase the pressure.

Just when she thought it wasn't going to work, the bubble burst. The orb providing light exploded when hit with a shard of metal from the cage. Luckily, the shields held, protecting them from the flying debris.

As the dust settled, Suleima released the shield surrounding her and Dynasira, picking her way the few steps to where she could feel Gage still locked behind his shield. She knelt carefully and pulled the shield down.

She could feel his pain as he limped to close the distance between them. She reached out with her right hand, burying it in his fur, laying her face on his neck, and breathing him in. Her relief consumed her.

Dynasira's disembodied voice reached them from the mouth of the tunnel, "We need to get moving guys."

The journey up seemed to take twice as long as the journey down had. But finally, they reached the top and solid ground to walk on. They walked back into the tree line and sank to the ground for a moment to rest. Gage pulled at the pack with his teeth and she allowed him to take it into the trees, his limp mostly gone.

She startled awake when a hand touched her cheek.

"We can't stay here. Do you need me to carry you?" Dressed in the jeans and shirt she had packed for him, his eyes had a bruised, sunken look, and his skin was pale, but he seemed otherwise unharmed to her inspection.

"I was so scared."

"That makes two of us." He touched his forehead to hers, breathing her in.

She couldn't break down yet, no matter how much she wanted to. "I can walk." She grit her teeth and stood, resting her head against Gage's strong shoulder for a moment to allow the pain to settle.

He kept the pack on his shoulder and carried her bow, keeping his other arm on the small of her back, ready to steady her as they began the hike back to the pack house.

"I can feel the pack. Those in the house when Kylin attacked," he said, "but they aren't there... I can't explain it."

"Kaly and the others are under some sort of spell. I didn't know how to break it and not hurt them. They are not being harmed, just kept out of it. I will get them out of it, I promise. I just needed to get to you. You were in immediate danger."

He stopped her. "I know you will. I'm not questioning any of your decisions. We can work together to figure this out." He made sure she understood he trusted her and her judgment, before dropping a quick kiss on her lips and turning to walk again.

Up ahead, Dynasira grumbled about her inability to fly them home. "You can't shift again until we can figure out how to get rid of that poison. I gave you a temporary fix, but it can't shift with you."

"Yeah, yeah," she grumbled back.

Gage stopped and tilted his head. Suleima paused, listening, and reaching out with her senses again. She had been scanning occasionally but to conserve what power she had left, she needed to use it wisely.

"Predators. A lot of them. Coming fast."

"In trucks and on dirt bikes. It's the pack," Gage said, relief evident on his face.

Dynasira nodded, picking up her pace to head them off.

"Sit," Gage ordered.

Suleima raised her eyebrows.

"Please," he amended.

She hesitantly sat at the base of a tree, Gage guiding her so she didn't jar her arm. He sat next to her, taking her uninjured hand in his.

"Don't scare me like that again," he said quietly. "I couldn't get to you. You were fighting. You were hurt."

"I'd do it again. You were taken. You were caged." She could feel his frustration building and released his hand to lay hers along his jawline. "If our roles had been reversed?"

"The world would still be burning," he replied without hesitation.

"Well, you know how I feel about fire," she responded, tugging playfully on the bit of beard he had been sporting lately.

He cracked a small smile. "You know I'm not going to let you out of my sight for the foreseeable future, right?"

"Yeah. Good thing you can't leave mine either."

The honking of a horn had Gage growling a moment later.

Chapter 26

WADE, THE SECOND IN command of the pack, dismounted from a dirt bike and head in their direction, two other dirt bikes, and an off-road pickup truck she had seen at the pack house before were right behind.

"Seems like you guys could use a ride," Wade said, grinning as Gage's growl could still be heard.

"Please." Suleima shifted her weight to stand, "How did you…"

"I knew something happened and headed straight to the pack house," Wade answered her unfinished question, "Found the fae lady at the house and the pack, well, you saw them."

She nodded.

"The fae lady gave me a general direction and said the waterfalls, so I rounded up the other pack members as they arrived. But it seems like we missed the fun!"

"There will be more fun to come, unfortunately," Gage said, steadying Suleima.

"But, we *really* appreciate the ride home," Suleima added.

Wade's gaze slid to Suleima's arm and Wade whistled and waved his hand in the air.

One of the pack members Suleima was not very familiar with jumped off another dirt bike and grabbed a bag from the bed of the truck.

"This is Ryan. He's been working alongside some of the jinn and healing shamans, training to do some first aid. Seems to be a high priority need recently." Gage stepped slightly to the side as he introduced Ryan.

"Nice to meet you," Ryan said shyly, "Can I check out your arm?"

Suleima nodded and attempted to pull her arm away from her body. If Gage had not caught her, her knees would have buckled beneath her. Gage growled violently, and Ryan flinched.

"Can you sit down, first," Ryan said quietly, carefully phrasing his words so they were not a command. "It will hurt, but if I can splint it until we get back, you will have an easier ride."

With help from Gage, Suleima sat back down. When Gage lowered himself beside her, still growling, she asked, "Do you need to move out of hearing range?"

She raised her eyebrows again when his lip curled in a snarl.

"No."

Ryan's hands shook as he reached for first aid supplies in his bag. And Suleima took in the wary look on Wade's face as he watched his Alpha.

"It will hurt more if he is shaking because he is afraid you will tear his head off for hurting her." Dynasira chimed in from the back of the truck.

Suleima turned to Gage. She could feel his rage, his frustration, and his wolf at the surface. She placed her hand on his jawline again and brought his forehead down to meet hers. She took a deep breath and waited for him to follow suit. He placed his hands on her hips, constantly tightening and loosening.

"They need to do this for me. I understand if you need to move away, out of hearing range. They will not hurt me more than needed."

"I am *not* leaving." His hands tightened again, almost painfully.

"Then I need you to focus on being calm and not growling at your friends," Suleima said calmly, melodically.

A low rumble sounded from deep in his chest.

"Better, but no. Do I need to have my dragon friend come and hold you down?"

"She'd be happy to do it!" Dynasira called from the back of the pickup.

Suleima turned her attention back to Gage, "What do we need to do to make this work?" Using precious little of her remaining power, she erected a ward around them, shutting all sound out but theirs.

"I wasn't there." His defeated voice broke her heart.

"It was my turn to save you."

His hands tightened again.

"Things are going to happen. Dirrin was apparently just the beginning. Our wolves are not trying to hurt me..." His gasp stopped her.

"Our wolves?" he asked.

"You are my mate, right? That hasn't changed, right?" His hands tightened again.

"Forever."

"Your pack is my pack. I protect them, as I will always protect you."

"I'm the Alpha. It's *my* job to protect."

"I'm not a shifter. I make my own rules."

"I won't leave," he said emphatically.

"Then what do we need to do to help you?" she repeated.

Gage shifted how he was sitting. He gently lifted her, placing her in his lap. His hands, back in place on her hips, tightened and loosened again. He lowered his head to her shoulder, his nose next to the bite mark he left.

Suleima felt his gradual relaxation. She waited a few more moments before speaking. "Ready?"

His hands briefly tightened.

"If you need us to stop, I'll do my best, okay?"

"Do *not* stop in the middle. It will hurt you more. Do *not* hide your pain from me. I felt you do it in the cave. *Never* hide from me." There was force in his voice, command, until he added, "Please."

"Together," Suleima said. "Together, you and I can do this."

She felt his slight nod, as he kept his head at her shoulder. She tilted her head, giving him easier access to their mark, and relaxed her neck, letting her head fall back against his neck and shoulder, releasing the ward and waving Ryan and Wade over.

Gage's hands stiffened as they approached, and she rubbed lazy circles on his thigh until he calmed.

"You—" Ryan's voice cracked, and he cleared his throat, "You may pass out from the pain."

A low rumble from Gage, but he remained relaxed.

"It may be a blessing if I do," she replied, lifting her head, "And Gage will allow you to finish whatever needs to be done." She patted his leg. "You will take me back to the pack house as quickly as you can, so I can sleep, right?"

Gage's voice was gravelly when he spoke, but it was clear, "I'll get you home." His hands tightened, he gave a slight nod, and everything went black.

Chapter 27

"How long was I out?"

"Most of the day," Zenisa answered.

"The pack?" Suleima asked, sitting up despite Gage's efforts to keep her where she was.

"Still under the spell, but no worse for the wear," Dynasira responded.

"And why is your hand still covered in poison? Are you unable to help her, Zenisa?"

Zenisa gave Dynasira a look before responding, "I am able to help her, but I need her to leave this room. There is recoil when nuckelavee poison is dispelled. She refused to leave your side."

"Go." Suleima pointed at the door. "I don't want to see you again until that hand is free of poison. And then we will discuss why you waited so long."

Zenisa smirked at Dynasira, before pushing her through the doorway.

Suleima started to rise from the bed, but Gage's arm snaked around her waist. "The pack is stable. We will get to that. First, you are going to sit here and allow Ryan to check over you and your wrist. Then, you will eat and regain some strength before you continue to try to save the world."

Suleima turned to see his face, her eyebrow nearly in her hairline.

His tone changed, almost pleading, "Please, let me take care of you. I need to make sure you are okay."

Suleima sighed. "I need to…"

"Take care of yourself in order to take care of others," Gage finished.

She huffed and was about to agree when a sudden, loud bang sounded outside. She slipped out of Gage's arms and was out the door and past Ryan, heading toward the stairs.

Gage's exasperated huff made it to her ears almost as quickly as he did. He lifted her in his arms, headed down the stairs and out onto the porch, refusing to loosen his grip on her.

Dynasira sat, stunned, in the middle of the yard and Zenisa laughed where she sat, halfway across the front yard.

Wade approached the porch. "Well, it worked," he said, shaking his head, pointing at Dynasira's hand she held up for everyone to see. "Blasted them apart, but it worked."

Suleima looked from Gage to the porch floor and back again, but he just tightened his grip on her.

"As much as I enjoy this, and I do," she said, "I'm capable of walking over to talk to Zenisa and Dyna."

"Not until Ryan can check you over."

Suleima huffed but did not argue.

"Why are you down here?" Dynasira asked as she approached the porch.

Suleima rolled her eyes.

Gage tightened his grip, dropped a kiss to her head, and smiled.

"Fine!" she said, pointing back to the door.

Gage's smile stretched across his face as he turned and carried her back into the house and back up to his room. He placed her back on the bed and sat next to her, as Ryan followed them in.

Ryan opened his supply bag and timidly looked up at Suleima. "How does your wrist feel?"

Suleima sat back in surprise for a moment before looking at her splinted wrist. "It doesn't hurt much now," she said, confused. "Pain medicine?"

Ryan shook his head, "We don't usually use pain medications, so I don't keep them on hand. The wolves heal quickly, and the meds don't usually work for us anyway." He reached for her hand but pulled away when Gage growled.

Suleima held up her finger for Ryan to wait a moment and turned to Gage. "We've been over this. Ryan needs to touch my wrist to examine it. It may cause me pain, but he doesn't mean to hurt me. If you want to stay, behave." She punctuated her statement with a quick kiss and motioned for Ryan to continue.

Ryan tentatively reached for Suleima's wrist. He carefully unwrapped the splint. While the wrist was tender, it hurt much less than it should have. Bruising struggled to show through the burn scars that covered her arm.

Suleima looked up as Zenisa entered the room. "I have been scanning you since you arrived with Gage. I think that unlocking your fae magic is also unlocking our healing abilities. It is still slower than us, still much slower than the wolves, but you are healing faster than a shaman would."

Ryan removed the splint entirely and Suleima tried to bend her wrist on her own. Her vision sparkled and she fought to stay conscious, and Gage's hold tightened around her.

Zenisa was at her side in an instant, "I didn't mean to try moving it! You are not healed yet. A wolf would still be tender right now, and you do *not* have a wolf's healing. The bone is knitting back together. The young wolf here has done a good job of setting your wrist, and it is beginning to heal, but you will still have a week or so before it is close to normal."

Suleima breathed through the pain as Ryan finished the exam and re-wrapped her hand and wrist. "As long as I don't bend it, it doesn't feel too bad." She held her hand up, examining the wrap when he finished. "But I guess the bow is out for a while."

"A long while," Gage replied, "You are lucky you aren't wrapped in bubble wrap."

She turned in his arms, "Same with you." She studied his face, his cheeks still more hollow, dark circles around his eyes, "Have you let anyone examine you?"

"I'm fine."

"So am I." She looked to Ryan, "Ignore anything he says. I am asking you to look him over and tell me that he is okay."

Ryan visibly swallowed before nodding.

"He would benefit from eating," Ryan said. "It's like he hasn't eaten for days."

"A result of Kylin drawing on his energy," Zenisa explained.

Suleima looked at Gage, "You have eaten since we got here, right?" When he didn't answer right away, she smacked his shoulder, "Eat, now. You want to yell at me and wrap me in bubble wrap. Not until you take care of yourself."

Chapter 28

Suleima finished eating before retrieving her bag of supplies to refill her elemental power wells. Despite her exhaustion, it was time to figure out how to free the pack from this spell. The weight of her fatigue pulled at her, feeling like her feet were weighed down with lead.

Gage stood in the corner to give her room to work. Zenisa sat on one side of Kaly, while Suleima sat on the other.

Suleima examined Kaly before speaking, "The spell seems weaker, but I still can't push through it."

Zenisa nodded. "This one seems to be on something like a timer. It is slowly dwindling. I suspect that if we leave it alone, it will dissipate in time. But how much time is the question."

"I will *not* allow them to sit within these spells for a moment longer than necessary."

"I agree," Zenisa said. "But to figure out how to break this spell, we need to understand how it was done."

Suleima nodded and re-examined Kaly more closely. From head to toe, she probed the bubble surrounding her, looking for weaknesses.

She squinted her eyes, before standing and walking out of Kaly's room and into the hallway. She reached out her uninjured hand and held it out from her hip, walking down the hall and into the next room, where another pack member lay. She retraced her steps back out after examining him and continued to each other pack member in the house who was affected.

When she finished, Suleima re-entered Kaly's room and sat down. "They're all connected," she said to Zenisa, "There's a trail, a string, of magic from each of the bubbles out into the hallway and leading to each of the other pack members."

"The spells are degrading at the same rate. I believe the spell was placed over all of the pack members at the same time. It would explain why there was so little resistance when Kylin entered the house and how she was able to take Gage without alerting the other pack members."

Gage spoke up, "I felt the ward go down. I was shifting when I felt the pack members in the house go… muted is the best word I can think of. I turned to head into the hallway when Kylin came into the room. I caught her off guard. I lunged at her from the side, knocking her into the lamp and breaking it. I knocked over the dresser when I went back at her a second time, but the moment I hit her, everything went black, and I only remember waking up in the cage in the cave."

Suleima turned to Gage, "Did any of the wolves who came to the pack house after I left scent anyone other than us in the house?"

Gage looked to Wade.

"Ryan and I were the only ones to enter the house after arriving. We scented the one in your room, sir. She went straight to your room and back out."

"Fae spells can be created in a few different ways. We can cast spells as you would do, Suleima. Or we can hold a spell in stasis. We attach it to an object which, once conditions are met, will release the spell. It could be released by someone non-magical, by the creator, or by simply having a timer expire."

"How would Kylin be able to break the ward, enter the house, and spell each of the wolves, except Gage, before anyone would react?"

Zenisa thought for a moment. "That points to a spelled object, something already in the house or on the property. As a vampire, she is fast, but having to subdue an unknown number of werewolves at the same time... It would be difficult for even her."

Suleima stood, steeling her resolve, and went back to examining the spell surrounding Kaly. She probed at the spell again using each of her elements, but none of them seemed to affect the bubble in any way.

"Talk me through what you are doing," Zenisa said.

Suleima explained what she was doing, and how she was able to break the spell holding Gage in the cage, explaining that she was trying to find a similar weakness within this spell.

Zenisa's face scrunched with concentration and Suleima felt her probing the bubble. Zenisa's frustration was clearly written on her face before she spoke absently. "There has to be some weakness, some way to release them."

A lightbulb moment for Suleima.

She stood quickly and rushed into the hallway again, a trail of people following in her wake, but giving her room. Keeping her good hand on the thread that led to Kaly, she followed it until it met with the next wolf. She moved her hand to their combined threads and followed it to the next, repeating it until she was at the top of the stairs, where each of the threads met.

Suleima wrapped the threads around her forearm and held the nucleus of the spell in her hand. She again probed at it with her elements, but the result was the same. She pulled the threads up, closer to her face, and watched it pulse, like nerves sending signals to each other.

Zenisa walked through the threads, causing the lightning pattern to stutter. She asked Gage to follow the same path. This time, the lightning shifted, reaching for Gage, before resuming after he had passed all the way through.

Suleima, still holding the nucleus, unwrapped the threads from her forearm and crossed through the threads herself. The threads wavered, almost reaching as they had with Gage, before retreating and stuttering as they had with Zenisa. She took hold of the thread coming from the last wolf, carefully peeling it from the rest of the threads, until it only connected to the nucleus. She pulled at the thread, causing the lightning to jump faster and more erratically, then let go of it, but it didn't rejoin the others.

As she watched, the lightning began to slow, as if weakened by being separated from the rest.

"Ryan, please go into that room and watch him closely," Suleima said, pointing to where the last wolf lay, "If he shows any sign of distress, tell me immediately."

Ryan followed her instructions and Wade moved to the door to relay any information, as Suleima continued to manipulate the threads.

Zenisa approached her, examining the threads as well. This time, when Zenisa touched the loose thread, it shivered and shied away from her.

At Suleima's direction, Zenisa grabbed the thread and slowly pulled at it, separating it from the nucleus entirely. The lightning flashed erratically before slowing, the length of the thread shortening. Zenisa kept it in her hand, walking toward the room that held the wolf, allowing the thread to retreat, but keeping it firmly in her grasp. Suleima followed her progress, watching for any change.

When Zenisa reached the foot of the bed, she released the thread. A loud pop echoed through the room, and the werewolf shot to his feet, ready to fight. The glow in his eyes told Suleima how close his wolf was to the surface.

Gage placed himself between Suleima and the newly awoken wolf. "Easy Ezra. The danger is gone. You are safe."

Ezra's eyes connected with Gage's, and he nodded stiffly, slowly sitting back down on the bed, taking in everyone and everything around the room. "What happened?"

"You were under a spell. Suleima and Zenisa were able to break it," Gage answered.

"Were you able to hear or observe anything while you were under the spell?" Suleima asked.

"I couldn't hear anything and I couldn't move. I couldn't find the pack. I was cut off from them." He tilted his head, thinking a moment before continuing, "Well, most of them. I could feel a few others. Others who were here at the house with us."

"So you can feel Kaly?" she asked.

"Well, no. Not now, but I could a few minutes ago."

"They're connected, we knew this. It's blocking their connection to the awake members of the pack, we knew this as well. But they have a connection still to the pack members who are spelled with them. Does any of this seem familiar? Do you know what kind of spell she used?"

"I don't..." Zenisa began.

"Think harder! My pack is trapped in this limbo!" she yelled.

Gage stepped out of the room. "Can you let go of the magic you are holding?" he asked Suleima quietly, but the Alpha power in his voice was evident.

She turned sharply at the command.

"Please," he said, softening his tone.

Suleima didn't want to follow him. She wanted to fix this. But, she also knew that she was being absolutely unreasonable. She gently released the bundle of threads and walked into Gage's bedroom as he guided her, his hand resting on the small of her back.

Gage sat on the edge of his bed, patting the spot next to him. He didn't speak until she sat. "I want you to close your eyes. Take a few calming breaths." His hand moved in circles across her back.

She did as she was asked, then turned to meet his eyes, icy blue ringed with violet.

"When we first shift and truly become pack, our emotions are heightened. We feel frustration and anger more keenly than before. When one of our pack is in danger, it's even more obvious," he said softly. "I understand your frustration and anger. I can feel it through our bond."

"I'm sorry," she started.

"There's no need to apologize," he interrupted. "I tell you these things because this is new to you. You have accepted my pack as yours. And while we are thrilled that you have joined not only me but this pack, we need to help you learn to channel and control your heightened emotions. Zenisa was less than thrilled at your frustration being directed at her."

Using it to ground her, she touched her forehead to his. Suleima breathed in his scent, the freshness of a run through the woods, mixed with a muskiness all his own. His hands rubbed up and down her arms, careful to stay above her injured wrist, adding to her calm.

When she opened her eyes, it startled her to find the room full of other wolves from the pack sitting along the edges of the room. She could feel their calmness radiating from them as it had from Gage.

Gage tilted her chin, meeting her gaze, "We'll help you. We have faith you'll figure out this spell. You will help our pack." He dropped a quick kiss to the end of her nose, then smiled, "Just try not to piss off the powerful fae goddess in the hallway, huh?"

Suleima nodded once, before standing and checking to make sure the hold on her emotions were solid. She rolled her neck and took the first steps toward the hallway, as the rest of the pack stood.

Ryan looked at her and smiled, giving her a thumbs up.

Wade stepped forward, "We've got you. And, you've got this."

Dynasira stood at the doorway and placed her hand on Suleima's shoulder as she walked through, adding her strength and confidence in Suleima to what she was already feeling from the pack.

Suleima approached Zenisa, "I apologize for my outburst," she said sincerely.

"The moment has passed. Shall we continue?"

Suleima walked a few more steps and picked up the threads of magic again.

Chapter 29

Each of the pack members were released one by one. When Kaly, the last pack member, was freed, despite being seemingly asleep for the better part of a day, her eyes drooped heavily.

Suleima turned to Zenisa. "They were a battery. Their own energy used to fuel the spell."

"It makes sense. It also makes sense that it was slowly dissipating. The werewolves have much higher stamina and energy than a human or shaman, but even they would run out eventually. And, as we released each wolf, they've been more tired. With fewer wolves to power the spell, it pulled more of the energy from the remaining wolves."

"In the end, it would have killed them."

"Unfortunately, it looks that way now, yes," Zenisa answered.

Gage's arms wrapped around her; her feelings of guilt must have bled through the bond, "They're safe now. We work with the knowledge we have and make decisions. We're all awake now. Focus on that."

Suleima steeled her spine and focused on Zenisa. "We have dismantled Kylin's spell seven times now, for each of the pack who were trapped in it. Do you have any idea if we could recreate it?"

"Why would you want to?" Dynasira asked.

Suleima turned to her, "Kylin feeds off of energy. If we recreate the spell and reverse it, make it so it pulls energy from outside of itself, could it pull energy from Kylin?

"It would take a long time to pull energy from Kylin, enough to hurt her at least."

"Not if we speed it up. If we can turn the spell inside out and place it on anyone who fights Kylin, if they let her get close enough, she would touch them, and try to drain them, right? So, we let her touch someone, but instead of making contact with their skin, she touches the bubble. Then we make it so the spell, when she initiates her siphoning of energy, the bubble reverses the siphon, and drains her instead."

"That might work," Zenisa said. "I need to check one of the texts in my home."

When Zenisa returned a few hours later, each of the spelled wolves had taken a short nap and were seated around the enormous dining room table, gobbling up the feast Suleima had spent the time preparing. She felt it as Zenisa passed through the ward she had replaced and stood from her spot at the table. She motioned to Gage to stay at the table, when he would have gotten up with her, and headed out the front door.

Zenisa met her in the center of the front yard. She held a large, leather-bound book under her arm. The binding was nearly worn through, and the scent of age and magic wafted from it, tickling her nose. "I think I have found a spell which is similar to the one Kylin used on the pack," she said. "I believe we can replicate it without difficulty. Altering it? That may be a bit of a challenge."

"Between the two of us," Suleima responded, "I believe we can figure it out." She turned and walked back up onto the large wrap-around porch of the pack house and dragged a heavy, rough-hewn log chair up to the matching, live-edge wood table.

Zenisa followed suit, before opening her tome and pointing at a page with strange writing on it. "This is written in our ancient tongue."

The characters seemed to swirl around the page, transfixing Suleima's gaze. One moment the symbols were still and the next they had rearranged themselves into something entirely new. "Why does it change?"

"You are not the owner. It's spelled to change and shift to keep the spells concealed inside safe from the eyes of any person, other than its true master."

Suleima felt a chill breeze swirl around her, could taste the ice on the wind as Zenisa channeled her power around the book. Before her eyes, the shifting of the characters ceased and settled into place, but they remained foreign to her.

"One day, when we are not facing down vampires and my sister, I can try to teach you some of our ancient tongue. The words are lost through time, but we can define what the characters mean in our modern language."

Zenisa continued, explaining the spell and how it worked. The spell was a ward, but flexible and powered from within the subject. She was still trying to figure out how Kylin was able to create the spell so it connected to each of the others. Each was a separate spell, tied and held together like a bouquet of balloons. And, how had she spelled them all at once?

"The wards I placed, before you taught me to entwine them with my fae magic and tie them off!" Suleima stepped away from the table and paced. "As I was taught, with shamanistic magic, the wards are not fully tied away from us. We must replenish them periodically, yes. But it's a constant, slow drain on our power wells. She was able to drain some of my power when she siphoned the magic in my ward. She is using a fae spell, somehow, as if it were shamanistic magic, and instead of tying it to herself, she is tying it to the wolves."

Zenisa thought for a moment. "That would make sense. Although her access to her shamanistic magic was severed with her natural death, I'm certain Solisa would not share her secrets of using magic with Kylin. She would strive to make sure Kylin knew enough, but not so much that she would become a threat to Solisa."

"How does that help us?" Dynasira asked from the doorway, moving aside to let Gage pass through.

"When I try to replicate her spell, I can tie it off. It won't drain on anyone who has the spell around them. It won't weaken them, or me." She stared out into the yard, her pacing stopped when Gage grabbed her hand, but her mind kept moving. She spoke to no one, her thoughts just spilling out, "If the spell is set to pull the energy from the person locked inside, if we figure out a way to invert it, in theory..."

"It would pull energy from the person who touched it from the outside," Gage finished when her voice trailed off. "But how do you keep her attached long enough for it to drain her energy?"

"I have a spell I've used in the past. I use my earth magic to grasp a person, like a hand of dirt. I've never used it in this fashion, but I should be able to do something similar with the ward, make it hold onto her when she touches it."

"And I have a way to speed up the energy siphon. It isn't complicated."

"How many of us can you put this spell on?" Gage asked.

"And how do we draw Kylin here?" Dynasira added.

"We won't need to. From what you and Suleima told me, Kylin was injured. I imagine that is the only reason why she is not here now. She would have known the moment Suleima and I broke her spells. As soon as she is able, she will be here. And, if we use an object to hold the spell in stasis, we should be able to put it on as many as we need."

Chapter 30

Suleima stood in the living room of the pack house; nearly a dozen wolves around her, including Gage, as well as Dynasira and Zenisa. "We don't need all of these people," Suleima protested.

"Our wolves would like to pay back Kylin for that spell she placed on them. I won't deny them that," Gage argued.

"More people means more people in danger," Suleima continued.

"Sul, you won't win this," Dynasira chimed in. "If she had put me or my dragons under that spell, you would not be able to keep us away."

"My people would feel the same," Zenisa added.

Suleima threw her hands up in the air, "Fine. But, everyone who goes will need the spell applied to them. I'm not taking any chances on losing someone."

Gage kissed the top of her head in front of everyone, making her blush, and smiled. "Agreed."

Soon everyone was piling in trucks with camping equipment and gear. No one wanted Kylin anywhere near the pack house again and

Suleima's cabin was barely big enough for her, let alone the crew of people insisting on going with her. They would head to the clearing where Suleima had trapped The Green Knight, and camp in the meadow.

Before long, a small tent city had emerged in the clearing with cozy campfires to cook and keep the evening chill at bay. And as darkness fell, Suleima felt more and more ill at ease. She left the cozy area, where the pack and Dynasira were talking and laughing, and walked to the tree line, out of the reach of any firelight. She gazed into the dark forest, just listening to the sounds of the woods around them.

"You okay?" Gage asked, walking up behind her and placing his hand at the small of her back.

"I don't think we will be here long," she said quietly, leaning into his warmth and wrapping her arms across her chest to ward off the unnatural chill she felt deep in her bones.

He pulled her into his arms and held her in the silence of the night. The comfort he offered was exactly what she needed. Her head fit perfectly on his shoulder, and she breathed in his scent, calming her further. Closing her eyes, it felt like they were the only two people there, wrapped in their own little cocoon, safe from the threat and chaos of the world around them.

Gage drew her lips to his in a kiss that left her knees weak and tears flowing. When he pulled away, he dropped his forehead to hers, "It'll be okay. We'll get through this together."

She tried but failed to smile. "The danger you and the pack have faced since I came here...," her words barely a whisper.

Gage lifted her chin with his finger, forcing her to meet his eyes, "I wouldn't change *any* of it."

She read the truth of his statement in his eyes and laid her head back on his chest, willing the world to stop for a bit, so they could just be.

Be here. Be alone. Be safe. She basked in the safety she felt wrapped in his arms.

All too soon, they heard light footsteps coming their way.

Zenisa headed their way with a handful of stones. "Your shamanistic magic needs to be replenished after using it. Also, we know that Kylin will be coming, but we have no idea exactly when. So, I brought these river rocks. These will act as our stasis conduits. I'll show you how to do this. The wolves will only need to activate them when Kylin shows up."

Suleima turned back to Gage. "Work calls," she said quietly.

He dropped a kiss to her nose. "Don't work too hard. I'll be over by the fire if you need me for anything."

The chill swept back over her as he walked back to the fire, but she blocked it out and focused on the lesson at hand. Suleima took a seat on the fallen log a few feet away and waited until Zenisa sat next to her. "This re-engineered spell will not harm my pack in any way, right?"

"It will be completely safe for them. We will be able to tie it off, so there is no effect on you or me either."

She nodded and watched carefully as Zenisa created the first spell, Suleima adding her shamanistic magic to make the spell latch onto Kylin when she touched it. With the first spell complete, Zenisa handed half of the stones to Suleima, and they worked side by side in comfortable silence creating each of the stasis conduits, only speaking if a question or correction was needed.

They had just finished the last of the conduits when Gage approached. He silently held out his hand and guided her to the tent they would use. Once there, he handed her the pack of supplies and backed away so she could prepare and complete her ritual to charge her power wells.

Finished, her eyelids grew heavy, but she carefully packed her supplies away and walked to each pack member to hand them the conduit stones and gave quick instructions on how to use them. "Hold it between your hands, if you are in human form. If you are wolf, grip it in your jaws. Rub the flat spot with your tongue or thumb three times, then add pressure by squeezing or biting the same spot. Those movements will release the spell. Do *not* approach Kylin without that spell engaged."

Chapter 31

A DISTANT HOWL WOKE her in the early hours of the morning. Kaly. Suleima was on her feet, just an instant behind Gage.

"She is coming in fast," Gage said urgently.

Suleima brushed the hair out of her eyes and exited the tent with her bow in her hand and arrows slung over her shoulder, pulling the arm guard carefully over her left wrist, hoping it would help support her injury when she had to pull back on the bowstring. In the clearing, each of the wolves were dropping the stones from their mouths and splitting off into the tree line around the clearing. Dynasira dropped her stone and shifted into her dragon form, taking to the skies. She felt Zenisa heading their way and turned to see Gage's wolf emerging from their tent. She dropped her own stone at her feet before heading into the trees as the other wolves had done, her first arrow at the ready. Despite the pain still present in her left wrist, Suleima refused to leave the bow behind.

Under the canopy of the trees, it was still dark, sunlight only fil-tering through the branches in a few spots. Suleima reached out with her senses. She was able to pinpoint the location of each of the pack members and sense Dynasira above. In the midst of it, the erratic and lightning-fast Kylin.

Suleima anticipated Kylin's movements and raised a root in her path, slowing her for a moment. It was then she sensed the second presence and turned back to the clearing. She stirred up the wind, shoving tents out of the way, then turned back to face the trees. She whistled for Dynasira and the wolves to get their attention.

She felt them heading back toward the clearing, but keeping to the trees surrounding it, harassing Kylin as she neared them, but keeping out of her reach. She looked up sharply at Dynasira's dragon screech. "Stay out of the fog released by the nuckelavees. It is toxic," she said. She didn't need to raise her voice to be heard. Not with the wolves' superior hearing. "There are more than one of them."

Suleima sent a wave of water at the tree line when the first line of nuckelavees reached the clearing. The nightmarish creatures walked right through the water without batting their single, blood-red eye.

"She's changed them!" Zenisa shouted, coming to stand next to Suleima. "Solisa must have changed them."

Suleima steeled her knees against the pain and fired an arrow at the front nuckelavee, hitting one of the unnaturally long arms from the human-like body protruding from its back. The reverberation of the bowstring sent ripples of pain down her arm, nearly dropping her to her knees. Ignoring the sparks in her vision, she steeled herself against the agony.

The nuckelavee released an ear-piercing wail before belching its toxic fog into the clearing.

Dynasira flew overhead, spitting boiling water onto the creature. Suleima pulled at the wind, blowing the fog up and out of the clearing.

Suleima sensed the pack in groups of two or three, harassing their own nuckelavees still hidden in the tree line. One would nip at its haunches before pulling back to avoid the fog, the next wolf approaching from a new angle, pulling the nuckelavee into a new position, away from the poison fog.

Gage took off into the tree line, but Suleima pulled her focus from him and back onto the problem in front of her.

Zenisa sent a spear of ice at the nuckelavee, hitting it in the front left shoulder of its horse-like body, causing it to rear back onto its hind legs. Suleima took advantage and fired another arrow, shifting it with air to make it hit directly in the chest. Where her wrist affected her aim, she compensated using her magic.

Time seemed to freeze as Dynasira spewed more boiling water over the nuckelavee and Zenisa froze the water solid around it.

"Fire again!" Zenisa shouted.

Suleima nocked and fired another arrow, pushing hard against it with air to increase its speed. Zenisa added ice to the arrow, changing its shape slightly. The arrow hit like a wedge and shattered the ice and the creature it surrounded.

Gage and three other wolves had taken down another of the nuckelavees in the woods, pulling it apart, and they were headed to help another group of wolves deeper in. There were still at least four other nuckelavees in the trees, and Kylin, who buzzed from place to place, probably looking for a weak spot to take advantage of.

Suleima ran and pulled at the earth, vines emerging from the soil and tangling through the legs and arms of a nuckelavee, restricting its movements. She wound a large vine around its neck and jaw, pulling its horse head down to the ground and clamping the jaw closed to keep it from releasing more fog. She then turned to head further into the woods, where Kylin seemed to be.

Zenisa and Dynasira were headed to another nuckelavee coming in from the north. The wolves were quiet as they fought, but the screams of pain and frustration coming from nuckelavees made concentration difficult.

A fireball flew by her, barely missing her face. The heat was so intense, she smelled singed hair. She quickly pulled a shield around herself and focused on Kylin. Suleima crouched, burying her fingers to the first knuckle in the earth, allowing her to get a better read on Kylin's movements. She tuned out the noise of the fight behind her and concentrated on Kylin.

Kylin and Dirrin had shared more similarities than just their affinity for fire. They both were easily taunted and angered. Suleima used that to her advantage. "Must you hide, Kylin?" she asked. "I'm about done with the trouble you are causing. If you want to destroy me so badly, come out here and do it."

Kylin's cackle echoed across the trees as she continued to bounce around at an unnerving speed.

Suleima dodged another fireball, snuffing the flames before any of the forest debris caught. "Is that your only trick? Yawn."

Two fireballs came at her from different directions. Suleima smothered the first and redirected the second back toward Kylin's latest location. A third came from behind and smacked into her shield, sizzling when it met the water. It weakened her shield, but she did not try to reinforce it; she would need to drop it completely before it was all said and done.

Suleima tripped her up again with an overgrown root and laughed when Kylin squealed in frustration.

A collective howl rose up. Someone was hurt. Badly.

This time, the fireball smacked straight into her shield, inches from her face. Suleima sucked the air away from it, starving the flames so they quickly burnt out, only to find Kylin standing in front of her with a maniacal sneer on her face. She startled and dropped her shield in the same breath.

Chapter 32

Suleima ducked away from the fist that Kylin swung her way on instinct, dodging behind her, but when the second shot came, she just waited.

She felt the moment the spell latched on to Kylin, saw her eyes widen with fear as the siphoning began. Suleima pulled hard at the earth, grounding her feet into the soft, loamy soil below.

The first thing she noticed was Kylin's cheeks; they began to have a sunken look which only grew more. Her eyes bulged. A smell of sulfur permeated the air.

Another second, and ash blew in the wind.

Suleima nodded sadly before walking over to Gage, kneeling and burying her hands and face in his fur. He was okay. The pack felt broken, but Gage was okay at least physically. She reached out with her senses and immediately knew, though no threat remained, one of their pack had been lost. The battle had cost them.

Suleima gathered her wits about her and stood, keeping her hand on Gage's fur, unwilling to lose that connection. "I'm going to get things cleaned up in the clearing," she said absently.

"We'll handle that," Dynasira chimed in, "You go back to the house with the pack. Zenisa and I have this covered, right?"

"Be with your pack, Suleima," Zenisa said, "You need to be together now."

Wade and Kaly ran ahead and the rest of the pack followed. Suleima's hand never left the fur on Gage's back as she slowed her pace to match his.

When her cabin came into view, Suleima sat on the porch and waited for him while he shifted and dressed.

Gage still didn't speak as they walked past the pack vehicles to the spot where Suleima kept hers. Gage opened the passenger door, tucking her into the seat and fastening her seatbelt, before walking around and climbing in the driver's seat himself.

His need to take care of her coursed through their bond so strongly; his turmoil at the loss of one of his pack warred within him. She released the seatbelt, ignoring his pointed look, and slid across the old bench seat. When she could move no closer without interfering with his ability to drive, she reached up and turned his face to hers, bringing his forehead down to meet hers.

He breathed deeply, taking in her scent, just as she was taking in his. The steering wheel creaked under the grip of his left hand. His right hand held hers tightly, but without the crushing tension he was putting her poor old steering wheel through. She brought their joined hands up, dropping a kiss to his knuckles, then another on the end of his nose before she sat back and curled into his side, resting her head on his shoulder, keeping their hands joined. Gage pulled her truck out onto the path and drove slowly, Wade and Kaly right behind. She did her best to keep feeding him calming energy and thoughts as they drove.

As he turned down the lane to the pack house, a sea of cars reflecting the sun's rays became visible in the distance. Gage pulled the truck to a stop and flexed his hand on the steering wheel again, before opening the door and climbing out.

Wade and Kaly stopped their vehicles and stepped out as the wolves in the back exited and headed into the house.

Gage's voice, much more gravelly than usual spoke up, "They'll shift. Then we'll meet inside."

Suleima nodded once, before being swallowed in his arms, his head buried in the crook of her neck. She held him just as tightly.

After a time, she asked quietly, "Who?"

"Ezra." His voice was barely a whisper.

A tear formed as she squeezed him just a bit tighter. "I'm sorry." The first wolf she had released from Kylin's horrible spell.

He pulled away just enough to look into her eyes. "You have nothing to be sorry for."

"I know. But I am sorry just the same," she said, giving him a sad smile. "I wish I had known him better."

Gage stepped away then but kept her hand in his. "They have shifted. We should get in there. You'll get a small piece of him now."

Together they walked into the pack house and into the large living room. Most of the seats were taken and pack members sat on every available inch of the floor as well. Gage took her over to the last remaining seat and sat, pulling her into his lap.

Suleima sat there for a while, listening to the pack tell stories about their fallen pack member, laughing and remembering the good times together. The smiles were genuine but sad.

Dynasira came onto the pack property, and Suleima made her way out onto the porch.

"Hey," Suleima said as she walked out onto the porch to greet her.

"Hey," she replied, "Zenisa and I took care of the remains of the nuckelavees." She motioned to a wood box placed on the bed of her old pickup truck, "I brought him, so the pack could decide where he should go."

Suleima pulled Dynasira into a hug. "Thank you. For everything."

"I'll go and let Agron know what happened and see to the rest of the council as well. Zenisa is headed back to the Phrostien Mountains. She will meet with her people and see what they are willing to aid with."

She gave her one last hug before watching Dynasira shift and head out. When she turned, Gage was standing on the porch, staring at her truck.

The pack filed out behind him and several walked around them, picking up the makeshift casket and carrying it back behind the house. Gage took her hand again and began to follow.

"I should stay...." she began.

Before Gage protested, Kaly stepped up to her, "You are pack. We do this as a pack." Kaly took her other arm, mindful of her injury, and the three of them walked solemnly behind the pallbearers, with the rest

They came to a spot nearly half a mile from the house, but still on Gage's property. A small copse of trees, most of them very young trees stood proudly in the area. A small memorial stood tall at the front. Suleima dropped their hands and walked forward on her own.

On the memorial were names and dates. Several were listed under the date of the battle with Dirrin. All of the fallen from their side that day were listed, thunderbirds, dragons, wolves, shaman. She traced her finger along the names.

"Pack or not, they were pack that day." Gage's hand settled on her back as he spoke.

She gave him a small, sad smile and took the hand he offered, then turned to face the pack.

She watched quietly as the pack prepared a blaze around the box they had lain on an already scorched piece of earth. No one spoke, just standing, mesmerized by the growing flames. Silent tears flowed over her cheeks as Gage led the pack, howling as the flames engulfed the box, only to be joined by their cousins in the wild in their sorrow song.

That night, most of the pack slept at the pack house. If there was a flat surface in the place, there was a human or wolf or both, sleeping on it. This newfound family was beginning to heal the hole left in her heart after the death of her mentor. She snuggled in closer to Gage's warmth and his arms tightened around her in response. She drifted off in peaceful slumber.

Nowhere near ready to awake, Suleima was left with no choice when she felt Dynasira land in the pack house yard with Agron right behind. Gage stirred right next to her and pulled her closer with a growl. She patted his forearm where it crossed over her stomach, holding her in place. "Dyna and Agron are here. I need to go and see what is going on."

He grumbled but let her up.

A few minutes later, as they stepped off the porch, Dynasira said, "We have news."

"What's going on?" Gage asked.

"Hamanad is missing."

"When do we leave?" Kaly asked.

"Soon."

Epilogue

While Gage met with Wade to prepare the pack for his leaving for an unknown amount of time, Suleima went for a walk to clear her mind and prepare herself for what was ahead. Listening to the birds' songs, she wandered aimlessly, guided by intuition alone.

Her feet carried her to the memorial of moonflowers. Suleima knelt in front of them and let the silent tears fall, giving in for a moment to the overwhelming feelings pressing down on her. So many losses, each of them weighing heavily on her heart. She sat quietly, losing herself in the beauty of the scenery surrounding her.

Sudden movement caught her eye. Halfway between where she knelt and the pond, a small vine moved toward the wind. She stood and walked over to the strange vine, kneeling again to better observe it. A set of eyes blinked up at her.

It was The Green Knight... or a...baby Green Knight?

The vine squeaked, reaching for her.

Suleima stretched out her arm, touching the end of the vine. It gently wrapped around her finger and pulled itself closer to her, stumbling on skinny stalks. There was no malice in the movements as it toddled closer. She looked around the area, searching for any other oddities, but found none.

The vine around her finger pulled tighter, then clumsily climbed into her hand.

Shock kept her immobile for several minutes before she heard rustling in the forest behind her. She didn't need to reach out with her senses to know it was Gage.

He stopped a few feet from her, seeing the creature in the palm of her hand, and looked at her quizzically.

She stood, bringing the creature with her, and closed the distance between them. "I think whatever Zenisa did to make those moonflowers grow so quickly... I think it made a new Green Knight sprout."

Thank you for reading my book! I hope you enjoyed it!! I'd love it if you would consider leaving me a review! Reviews can help convince another reader to give one of my books a try.

My imaginary friends aren't done yet. I hope you come back to see the exciting conclusion to this storyline in Elements & a Key! Suleima and friends will return with more adventures and action as they search for the key and their friend, Hamanad, in a frantic bid to find it before the Sun Goddess, Solisa. What new friends will they find along the way? I know I can't wait to find out, so I better get writing!

Haven't joined my mailing list yet? What are you waiting for? You are missing out on the freebie prequel scene where you get to meet Erist, *alive*! And the prequel novella Elements: A Battle Before. The novella tells the story leading up to and including the battle against Dirrin *before* the start of Elements & Flame, where Dirrin and Suleima battle to a draw, both of them too injured to continue. You can get both for free by going to www.jillianbeane.com and signing up for my newsletter. As a newsletter subscriber, you will get updates on current and upcoming projects and will be the first to see new covers and release dates!

About Jillian

JILLIAN HAS BEEN WRITING since high school. Finally published 25+ years later, she has had oodles of careers to keep her busy along the way....

Stay-at-home mom

Preschool Teaching Assistant

Licensed Journeyman Plumber

Secret Squirrel

Security for a Professional Baseball Team

Disability Adjudicator

Credit Card Fraud Investigator

Does she know what she wants to do when she grows up? Nah! Where's the surprise in that?!?!

Surrounded by the support of her loving husband, her two amazing and crazy kids and her family, she is adding AUTHOR to her ever-growing list of careers.

When she isn't writing, you can find her reading, watching movies, listening to music, or hanging out with her Yas at their favorite art studio getting into ALL the shenanigans. Whether creating with her words or her hands, Jillian finds joy in art of all forms, be it remodeling or building homes, crochet, painting on canvas or pottery, or simply sitting in front of the dreaded blinking cursor, preparing to go on an adventure with her imaginary friends.

Acknowledgements

First, thank you to all of you who have read this book through to the end. Thank you for coming along on this journey with me! I truly hope you enjoyed it. Hopefully there will be many more adventures together in our futures!

This book would have never been possible without the support of my amazing husband and beautiful daughters. I can never thank them enough. To my husband, my first alpha reader, thank you for helping to bounce story ideas off of and helping me identify my 'that' and 'all' problems— and all the problems that have yet to be identified!

To my Yas, I cannot express how much your support and cheerleading helped to get me through the imposter syndrome moments. And a special thank you to the QueenYa for all of your help in 'fixing' my attempts to create a cover, logo, bookmark, etc. and advice on creating my small business! As always, the covers shine after being in your masterful hands!

To my Author Ever After community, thank you for lighting the fire under me and helping to walk me through the intimidating process of self-publishing.